A MUTUAL ATTRACTION

Browning smiled, pulling Alexandra closer so that she was once again aware of the fragrance of bayberry, blending with that of the blossoms and newly mown grass. It was a heady scent, and she felt herself yielding.

"And what of you, Miss Lytton?" he asked, his breath warm upon her cheek. "Would you love to go to the fair with me?"

Alexandra caught herself just in time and slipped out of his arms. "Naturally I shall love going to the fair with you and the children."

Her voice was bright and she hurried to collect the basket. More than one governess had found herself in trouble for forgetting the line between herself and her employer. She did not plan to be such a one.

"I will tell the children and we will be ready shortly, sir." She called to him over her shoulder as she hurried toward the manor, eager to put as much distance as possible between them.

Browning stood and watched her go, the skirt of her red gown moving gently in the spring breeze. He shook his head to clear it. Once again he told himself that he was most fortunate that Miss Lytton was a sensible woman, and once again he wondered what had happened to the self-control upon which he had prided himself for so long . . . .

Books by Mona Gedney

A Lady of Fortune

The Easter Charade

A Valentine's Day Gambit

A Christmas Bethrothal

A Scandalous Charade

A Dangerous Affair

A Lady of Quality

A Dangerous Arrangement

Merry's Christmas

Lady Diana's Daring Deed

Lady Hilary's Halloween

An Icy Affair

Frost Fair Fiancé

A Love Affair for Lizzie

The Affair at Greengage Manor

Published by Zebra Books

THE AFFAIR AT GREENGAGE MANOR

Mona Gedney

ZEBRA BOOKS
Kensington Publishing Corp.
http://www.zebrabooks.com

ZEBRA BOOKS are published by

Kensington Publishing Corp.
850 Third Avenue
New York, NY 10022

All Kensington titles, imprints and distributed lines are available at special quantity discounts for bulk purchases for sales
promotion, premiums, fund-raising, educational or institutional
use.

Special book excerpts or customized printings can also be created to fit specific needs. For details, write or phone the office
of the Kensington Special Sales Manager: Kensington Publishing Corp., 850 Third Avenue, New York, NY 10022. Attn.
Special Sales Department. Phone: 1-800-221-2647.

Zebra and the Z logo Reg. U.S. Pat. & TM Off.

First Printing: August 2004
10 9 8 7 6 5 4 3 2 1

Printed in the United States of America

PROLOGUE

Alexandra smoothed the silken skirt of her gown and looked about the ballroom, enjoying the music and the dancing candlelight. She knew very few people here tonight, and she did not expect to be asked to dance.

As the strains of a waltz floated through the room, she began to sway slightly, humming to herself. Suddenly she realized that a dowager in turban and feathers was watching her with amusement, and she flushed slightly. Then, deciding she wouldn't deprive herself of the joy of dancing simply for lack of a partner, she withdrew to a curtained recess. There she gave herself happily to the music, whirling about the alcove with her eyes closed.

Midway through the dance, someone clasped her waist and took her right hand firmly in his left. Her eyes flew open, and she was looking into the dark eyes of a gentleman of commanding presence who was, amazingly enough, even taller than she was. Dark winged brows above dark eyes and a Roman nose put her immediately in mind of an eagle, and she wondered for a moment if she were the prey.

"I heard you humming and looked in. I could not resist," he said, and she nodded to herself. The movement of the prey and the descent of the eagle—it was a pattern as old as nature herself.

"May I ask why you are nodding?" His eyes were bright with curiosity.

"It seemed to me, sir, that you are very like an eagle, swooping down upon its prey," she responded, smiling up at him.

He returned the smile warmly, and Alexandra noticed approvingly that his smile was reflected in both his eyes and voice.

"If you imagine me to be an eagle, ma'am, just how do you see yourself? As a bright-scaled fish slipping down a stream, unaware of the lurking danger? As a timid rabbit venturing forth from her burrow?"

"A hedgehog would be closer to the mark, I believe, sir—so you see that I need not fear you."

His smile deepened. "I consider myself forewarned."

She smiled back at him, but then gave herself to the music once more, not speaking. He danced gracefully, his movements sure. As the final strains of the music faded, he lifted her hand to his lips—very carefully.

"I am most indebted to you, dear lady, for the pleasure of the dance—and the conversation. Despite my likeness to a predator, will you grant me the next dance as well?"

Alexandra considered the matter a moment, then nodded. "Since I have the security of my prickles, I believe I may safely do so."

"Then I will ask the players for another waltz." Bowing, he turned and slipped out through the curtains.

A moment later the curtains parted again and she looked up, her heart quickening gladly. It was not her dancing partner, however, but a footman sent to find her.

"Miss Lytton, your presence is requested upstairs," he said, bowing.

Alexandra followed him slowly up the stairs, glancing about the ballroom as they left. She did not see the gentleman again, but as she reached the top of the stairs, she heard the lilting melody of another waltz.

CHAPTER 1

Richard Browning sat comfortably in a pale wash of spring light, his long legs stretched before him. He glanced with satisfaction from the flawless gloss of his top boots to the pleasant prospect of his sunlit, manicured gardens. Everything was well kept and orderly; even the charming wilderness was screened from view by box hedges and stone walls. Beyond the gardens, an impeccably groomed sweep of green lawn rolled gently down to the edge of distant orchards, now a foaming sea of blossoms. The plums from these orchards lent their name to Greengage Manor.

Beyond the plum trees stretched more orchards of cherries and apples, the fruit of which would supply the manor with preserves and jams, cider and brandy. Even from this distance he could feel the invitation to linger in their fragrant groves. The scene before him must look, he thought, much as Eden had appeared to Adam.

If Browning was complacent, he could perhaps be forgiven. After all, he had reached the enviable state when everything in his life was at last precisely as he had always wished it to be. Indeed, he thought, smiling as he turned toward the sound of Pamela's voice, such perfection had been well worth the years of longing and unhappiness. All of that was well behind him, and the future promised only happiness.

"Richard? Richard, where are you? I need to speak with you now, please." Her voice, though light and girlish, had the unmistakable ring of authority. It was a voice that demanded immediate attention.

Browning, pleased to have someone calling him and in need of his help, obediently rose and strolled into the drawing room through the French windows, which he had left open to the seductive spring breeze. The room before him, a confection of cream and gold, served as a most effective setting for Pamela Wingate. Her flaxen curls seemed to belong there, an integral part of the designer's plan, and her gown, a pale green muslin patterned with small yellow flowers and tied high under the bosom with a yellow sash, could have been artfully chosen to wear in this very room—as indeed it had been.

Browning paused to study the effect appreciatively. "You look delightful, my dear." He took her hand and pressed it lightly to his lips. "You are an ornament to my drawing room and my life." He had long been a master of courtly compliments, and this one came easily as he looked down at her.

Pamela reclaimed her hand and dimpled at him prettily, then spoke in the same manner in which she would have humored a child who had shown her a drawing of a stick figure and asked if she admired it. "A very pretty speech, sir—although I daresay you meant to say *our* drawing room."

The sharpness of her tone and words were so much at odds with her delicate appearance—and with her customary manner—that Browning stopped short and looked at her more closely. Pamela, however, took no note of his surprise at this quick dismissal, for she had turned her attention once more to the paper she was holding.

"But now we must be serious, Richard. There are decisions still to be made about our dinner party this evening."

Browning, weary of the subject, shrugged lightly and turned back toward the open windows once more, allowing his gaze to linger on the lacework of the distant blossoms. It seemed to him that their perfume was drifting lightly into the room, even at this distance. The orchards were, as they had long been, a source of comfort and joy to him. For him, Greengage Manor had always been a magical place. He hoped that Pamela too would soon fall under its spell.

"What great decisions must yet be made, my dear? I have given you the guest list, we have sent the invitations, and all plan to attend. The menu is planned and the cook alerted. What remains to be decided?"

"Why, the seating at table, of course, and determining who will escort whom in to dinner."

She looked at him with rising exasperation, grateful that the menu indeed had been decided. At her urging, that had been settled days earlier, and the necessary supplies had been packed into the baggage coach that had followed them from London.

They had made quite a satisfactorily impressive procession, she had thought—she and her mother and Richard in the handsome lead carriage, followed by a coach carrying her abigail and that of her mother, Richard's valet, and Butterworth, the elderly butler who managed both Browning's London home and Greengage Manor. Third had come a lumbering coach weighed down with the baggage that had not fit on the first two, along with all of the necessary household supplies that could be purchased only in town.

Butterworth had painstakingly ordered what was needed for the manor, as he always did, but Pamela had visited countless shops and added a substantial number of boxes to their baggage. After all, she had explained, next month there would be the house party, so it was necessary to plan ahead. It was just as well that at least one of them was willing to do so.

"Have you not given the matter of dinner partners any thought at all, Richard?" Her voice expressed clearly her disbelief at such an oversight.

"But what is there to think about, my dear?" he inquired patiently. "This is not a grand ball. It's only a small party for a few old friends who are eager to meet you."

His eyes grew soft as he looked down at her small, intent face. "And they will naturally be so delighted to make your acquaintance that they will pay no attention to such trifling matters as who their partners are at dinner."

For a moment Pamela paused, tempted to allow herself to enjoy his compliment and to return it in kind, as she had during their courtship. Then, however, she remembered the importance of the matter at hand and returned to it with determination. Although she was small and deceptively fragile in appearance and manner, Richard was discovering that his fiancée was capable of being distressingly single-minded.

"I should imagine that you will escort Lady Trillby," she continued, studying her list intently, "and that Sir Lionel will escort me, for they are the guests of highest rank. But what of Mrs. Damson and Miss Wentworth and Mrs. Pendergrass? I know nothing of them nor their standing in society. Which of the remaining gentlemen should escort each of them? And who should my mother's partner be?"

Seeing that she was not to be distracted, Browning resigned himself gracefully to matters domestic rather than matters romantic, and together they sat down to pore over the short list of guests and determine the arrangements for the dinner party. He soon discovered, though, that his mind still had a tendency to wander, even when he was removed from the distraction of the windows.

Instead of the orchards, however, he now watched Pamela, again noting with pleasure the fetching contrast of her gown against the pale golden glow of the sofa's brocade. She could have been posing for her portrait, so elegantly had she arranged herself against the cushions, so gracefully did she hold her head a little to one side so that her small, sculptured features were displayed to best advantage.

He was, he knew, a most fortunate man. Not only was he master of his beloved Greengage Manor, but also, once he had decided that it was at last time to marry, he had encountered the perfect young woman almost immediately. As dainty and fair as a porcelain shepherdess, Pamela Wingate was also intelligent and very efficient—and she had been his fiancée for a highly satisfactory fortnight. Shortly he would be holding a ball in London to announce their engagement officially, and then he would be hosting a house party here at Greengage.

It was impossible for her to make his life better ordered than it had been, for he was a meticulous man, but Pamela had devoted herself to making it busier. From the time she had accepted his offer, his days had become a succession of dinners, breakfasts, balls, theater visits, social calls, and shopping expeditions, all of them carefully orchestrated by Pamela and her mother.

He had no real objections to this arrangement, as long as it did not last indefinitely, and so he had indulgently allowed her to plan each day, down to the minutest detail, not leaving himself enough time even to ride in the Park or to go to his club. He had told her, however, that he wished for her to visit Greengage Manor before the time of the house party. She was, of course, familiar with his town house in Mayfair, where he spent a portion of each year, but the majority of his time was spent at his country home.

Although she much preferred life in London, Pamela had been eager to see Greengage Manor, the estate of which she would soon be the mistress, and she was equally eager to make her first mark in country society there. On this first trip, they did not plan to stay more than a few days before returning to London and continuing with the preparations for the ball and the house party. At first making a trip to Greengage before the house party had seemed nonsensical to Pamela, but Browning, anxious to be home at blossom time, had told her that he wished to give a small dinner party so that she could meet a few of their neighbors before the festivities of the house party. Determined that her first dinner party at Greengage would be perfect, Pamela had begun planning it immediately.

The invitations for the dinner had been sent from London, and the affianced couple, accompanied by Mrs. Wingate, had arrived at Greengage Manor only the evening before. Although she did not expect callers that day, Pamela had surveyed the drawing room upon their arrival and had today arrayed herself appropriately for receiving guests in that chamber. It was, she thought, important to begin life here just as she planned to have it continue. She wanted all concerned to recognize clearly that she was the mistress of the manor and a lady of elegant taste.

Once the matter of dinner partners had been satisfactorily settled, she laid her list aside and turned to him once more. "I have already spoken with Cook about tonight's dinner," she informed him, her tone mildly dissatisfied.

"Have you indeed?" he asked, startled. "I thought that Butterworth had made all the arrangements with Mrs. Melling."

He did not add that Pamela was not accustomed to

supervising a household staff nor that Butterworth and Mrs. Melling had managed Greengage Manor very capably for years.

"He had done so, but I wanted to see the recipes that she planned to use for the rabbit curry and the sauce for the capon. If those dishes are poorly prepared, they are quite inedible."

"But Mrs. Melling is an excellent cook, my dear," he protested, knowing how surprised that lady must have been to be called from her busy kitchen and questioned about her cookery on the morning of a dinner party. "I'm certain that you can safely entrust the dinner to her and Butterworth."

"So she told me," responded Pamela, her voice sharp. "And I am not accustomed to encounter such a high-handed manner in servants, Richard."

He looked at her in some dismay. "Mrs. Melling, high-handed? I'm sure she was merely trying to assure you that you need not worry about this evening, Pamela. She is truly the pleasantest of women."

Pamela looked unmoved. "I need no reassurance from my servants, Richard—nor will I allow my dinner to fail because I have not instructed them properly."

At her final words, the furrows in Browning's forehead relaxed and he patted her hand. "Your dinner will not fail, my dear. I know that you're nervous about this evening, but you need not be. Our guests will be delighted with you and delighted with the dinner. You need only enjoy yourself and leave this first affair entirely to Butterworth and Mrs. Melling. You may rely upon them."

Pamela had every intention of continuing her conversation with the cook but, recognizing that he had been unsettled by her comments, she wisely did not mention that to him. She had no wish to upset him just

now. Capturing Richard Browning had been a significant victory for her. Not only was he a man of property
and fortune, but he was also as striking a figure as any
woman could have wished, tall and gypsy dark. A perfect foil for her pale golden beauty and delicate figure,
she had thought with satisfaction. And he was quite as
elegant in his tastes as she was herself. She never could-
have allowed herself to marry someone who lacked
discriminating tastes.

After their first introduction, she had courted his attention carefully, without allowing herself to appear too
eager. Browning was a favored guest of hostesses of the *ton*,
for he was a man of excellent address and gracious manners. She had managed to be invited to one of the more
intimate dinners that he attended, and the two of them
had spent a delightful evening discussing their travels. He
had then sought her out at the Stamfords' ball the next
evening and had danced with her twice, and the following
day he had called upon her, sent flowers, and invited her
and her mother to the theater. His proposal had come as
a surprise, nonetheless, for he was still a bachelor at thirty-
five, and the mothers of marriageable young women had
given up hope of capturing him some time ago.

Once engaged, however, Browning had proved to be
surprisingly pliable, with the exception of his desire to
visit Greengage Manor before the time of the house
party. However, since she had been as eager to see it as
he was to show it to her, this had presented no problem.
It was, he had told her, the most beautiful place on
earth—and the dearest to his heart. To Pamela, Greengage Manor meant that she would be mistress of both a
house in Mayfair and a gracious home in the country.
The possession of Greengage Manor added substantially
to her own importance.

When she had seen it first yesterday evening, she had

been very pleased. If the manor house was very modest when compared to large and imposing houses such as Blenheim or Chatsworth, it was nonetheless unmistakably lovely. She had seen with satisfaction, too, that the manor's window tax must be gratifyingly high, for as they drove up the carriage sweep to the front door, she had counted more than twenty windows across the front of the house alone.

"How charming a place this is, Richard," she had said admiringly, putting one small gloved hand on his sleeve. "You must have been very happy living all your life in such a place."

She had felt his arm stiffen slightly, but he had replied easily enough, "Indeed, my dear, as I have told you, there is no happier place to live than Greengage Manor. Our children will love it here."

Pamela had felt a ripple of distaste at his remark. She knew, naturally, that she must in due course provide him with an heir, but her view of the future did not include living a bucolic life surrounded by children. She planned to become a hostess of consequence in London, and when she and her husband came to their delightful country home for a few brief stays during the year, they would bring guests to enliven their days. For her, the house party they would soon be giving was a foretaste of their married life.

Of course, a child—or possibly, if she were unfortunate, children—would of necessity live here with the appropriate nurses and governesses to oversee them. At that thought, she relaxed once more. Of course any children would stay here—or they would until they were old enough to be sent safely to some remote boarding school. She need not be troubled by their presence.

She had smiled up at him. "Of course they will be happy here, Richard. How could they be otherwise?"

And now, noting his distress about Mrs. Melling, she once again smiled up at him, forcing herself to give way to his wishes. "I am certain that you are correct, Richard, and that Butterworth and Mrs. Melling will see to everything."

Browning lifted her hand to his lips. Small, white, and soft, it was as perfect in every detail as she was herself.

There would be time enough, she thought, to see to Butterworth and Mrs. Melling. The butler was old, after all, and Mrs. Melling too could be replaced. Such changes could be made quite easily after her marriage.

The dinner was a great success. As Browning had assured her, his neighbors were prepared to be charmed by Pamela, and charmed they certainly were. She was an attentive, gracious hostess, treating each of them as a valued friend.

Having questioned Browning closely about their habits, she was careful to see that Lady Trillby had an extra helping of the muffin pudding for which she had a weakness and that Sir Lionel was provided with a footstool to ease the pain of his gouty right foot. She chatted about children and spring fashions with Clara Damson and listened, smiling, to Matthew Damson's interminable stories of the hunt.

When the ladies left the gentlemen to their port and retired to the drawing room, Mrs. Pendergrass was touched to see Pamela place a fire screen to protect her guests' complexion from the heat, and Miss Wentworth was delighted by the appearance of her favorite lemon biscuits with the evening tray of coffee and tea.

"You performed splendidly tonight, Pamela," Mrs. Wingate assured her daughter after the last guest had departed. "They adored you."

Although she was quite as small as her daughter and certainly as pale, her appearance differed in a few significant ways. Where Pamela's mouth was a graceful rosebud, her mother's was a small, thin slit. Pamela's eyes were the same pale, cool blue, but her mother's eyes looked hard, as though they had frozen in place. Browning had gradually become aware of these differences, and he was grateful that his fiancée was a much gentler version of her mother.

Pamela sank gracefully onto the closest sofa and put her hand to her forehead in mock anguish.

"I am certainly grateful that the first evening is behind me," she said lightly. "One never knows how country folk will react to a newcomer, but even that pitiful Mrs. Pendergrass seemed to accept me."

"Pitiful?" said Browning, frowning a little. "In what way is she pitiful? I have always been fond of Mrs. Pendergrass."

"Did you not note how antiquated her gown was, Richard?" Pamela's delicate brows arched in surprise. "I am amazed that you did not see it when you are so discerning! And the only jewelry she wore besides her earbobs was that odd gold brooch holding a bit of plaited hair."

"In memory of her late husband." His voice was stiff. "And I confess I had not noted the age of her gown." Browning studied his fiancée, still frowning. "She was a dear friend of my grandmother, and she has always been kind to me."

Pamela caught her mother's warning glance and smiled at him prettily. "But of course such things as dress do not matter when one speaks of such a friendship." Her voice was suitably contrite. "I am certain that I shall soon come to value her just as you do. I can't think how I came to speak so foolishly."

"You are overtired by your exertions, my dear," said Mrs. Wingate swiftly. "You are not yourself."

Browning's expression relaxed and he looked instantly remorseful. "Of course you are tired, Pamela. I keep forgetting how new all of this is to you. You have had the trip from London and the strain of meeting a group of strangers who will be important to you in your new life here." He took her hand and pressed it to his lips. "Am I forgiven?"

Pamela smiled gently. "Only if you can forgive me. It was my odious remark that began all of this."

He shook his head. He reproached himself for his continual failure to remember how young she was and how unfamiliar his world here was to her. "I have not thought of your comfort as I should have, Pamela. I fear that I have been too accustomed to thinking only of my own pleasure."

"You are too hard upon yourself, Richard. You know that I am delighted to be here at Greengage Manor with you." Her blue eyes brimmed tenderly as she looked at him.

"I promise that I shall do better," he replied firmly. "Tomorrow I shall begin to make amends."

Long after Pamela and Mrs. Wingate had retired that evening, Browning paced up and down the terrace. Late in the winter just past, he had decided to marry before another year slipped by. He knew that his grandmother would have wished him to do so, and she had been often in his thoughts during the past few months. Without her, his life would have been a very different one, and he was grateful to her.

He had been thinking, too, of how different a life he would have once he married. He would have a companion and eventually he would once again have a family, and he had found himself wishing for that comfortable situation during the long winter evenings. He had been as busy with friends and activities as he normally was, yet he had recognized that something was lacking.

Occasionally he thought of the delightful young woman with whom he had once waltzed and who had had vanished without a trace. He sometimes found himself watching for her at large affairs, but he had never again caught even a glimpse of her. Undoubtedly, he had decided, she had found his company unattractive and had retired before he could return. Finally he had decided that this spring he would find a pleasant young woman of good family, marry her, and set up his own family at Greengage Manor.

When he met Pamela, she had seemed particularly well suited to him. She had tastes similar to his own, she was a charming companion, and she seemed to be fond of him. An additional advantage, one that he had just realized since their return to Greengage Manor, was that there was nothing in her appearance to remind him of those who belonged to his past.

The bright light of a full moon had turned the landscape into a scene from a fairy tale, and he gazed at it with affection and gratitude. Everything before him seemed glazed in silver, offering a wealth that was to be prized far beyond ordinary riches. In the distance lay the orchards, their comforting presence offering an anchor in an insecure world, just as they always had.

He would give no more thought to the young lady who vanished. And he would not allow himself to think of his parents or of his life before coming to Greengage Manor—but involuntarily his hand went to the pocket of his waistcoat, in which he always carried a small gold case containing two miniatures. When he realized what he had done, he patted it absently without removing it and shook his head. The past was dead and gone. He had turned his face firmly toward the future.

CHAPTER 2

"Claire, I can't find Michael. Do you know where he is?"

Clarissa looked up from her book, surprised by the sharpness in her sister's voice. Isobel seldom raised her voice or grew impatient, no matter what the provocation. And with Michael, much as they all loved him, there was usually considerable provocation.

Clarissa shook her head and carefully put her bookmark between the pages so that she wouldn't lose her place. "Not for an hour or two, Belle," she replied. "I should imagine he'll be back in time for supper, though."

Then, seeing her sister's expression as she glanced at Jennifer and Ned, who had looked up at the mention of supper, she added hurriedly, "I'm certain he'll be here soon." Clarissa knew that their supper would be marked only by the sinking of the sun. There would be no food. The younger two were not aware of that, however.

"Isn't it time for supper, Belle?" asked Ned longingly. "We haven't had anything since breakfast, and it's ever so long since then."

As usual, Jennifer didn't say anything, but she watched Isobel closely, her dark eyes large in her thin face. She was holding her satchel tightly, their grandmother's diary clutched in one small hand.

"And there wasn't really very much to eat for breakfast," continued Ned, who believed in speaking the truth as he saw it. "We each had scarcely a bite or two of bread, and that was dry and crumbly."

"I know we're all hungry, " Isobel replied regretfully, "but I'm afraid that we might have to wait until morning before we can eat again."

Looking at their forlorn faces, she did not add that she could not see how the arrival of morning would help them. She had used their last bit of money for the loaf of bread that she had portioned out so carefully, and they had finished that at breakfast. Since then she and Michael had been racking their brains to think of what they might do next. She had nothing left to sell, and they still had miles to go. They were all footsore, even though a cart had brought them along the last twenty miles.

Just now, however, she discovered that fear and anger could drive out hunger very effectively. She could not imagine where Michael might have gone. After the kindly cart driver had let them out and turned down a quiet country lane toward his home, they had found this deserted, tumbledown cottage quite by accident.

The five of them had gathered enough wood to start a comfortable fire to ward off the chill of the spring night that would soon be upon them. In the late afternoon sunshine, the children had wandered in the overgrown garden and fields around the house. Isobel had been hopeful that they would find something edible, but thus far they had had no luck.

The others had finally grown tired of wandering and had come to join Clarissa, who had been reading on the doorstep of the cottage, taking advantage of the last lingering rays of sunlight.

But Michael had disappeared.

"Well, let's go in and build our fire," said Isobel with a false brightness. "And we can arrange our pallets in front of it. It will be the coziest place we've slept in quite some time. No hedgerows or spinneys for us tonight."

"But what about Michael?" asked Ned, growing alarmed at these preparations for bed when their brother was still absent. "He should be here, too."

Indeed he should, thought Isobel bitterly. Who could imagine what Michael might be doing? He had always been as unpredictable as the weather, and now, when they needed him most, he had chosen to disappear. She was resolved to ring a peal over him whenever he returned. This time he would not escape scot-free after his escapade.

The four of them had just grown comfortable in front of the fire when they heard a sound at the doorway.

"Michael?" Isobel sat up abruptly. "Is that you?"

"Who else?" he inquired cheerfully, coming close to the fire and opening his pack. "And just wait until you see what I've brought for everyone."

"What? What do you have?" demanded Ned, as all of them crowded close about him. "Is it something to eat?"

"But of course it is," he assured them, pulling out a plump brown fowl and pulling off the drumsticks and handing them to Ned and Jennifer. "How could you doubt that we would have supper? And not just *any* supper, mind you, but one that is quite delectable."

The two of them settled down to the serious work of eating while Michael laid out the other parts of their picnic. He had a fresh loaf of bread, some boiled eggs, five potatoes baked in their jackets, and a sausage.

"Where did you get all of this?" demanded Isobel in a whisper, having pulled him off to one side. "How did you pay for it?"

Michael hugged her lightly and patted her on the cheek. "You worry far too much, dear Belle. Just trust me—I have found a guardian angel for us."

Isobel was unable to ask him anything more, for the other three—even Clarissa, who was now eating a wing of the fowl—descended upon him once more.

"Tell us where you got all of this, Michael!" they pleaded. "How did you manage it?"

"Well, the cart driver had told me about an inn," he began, "an out-of-the-way inn called The Bull and Basket." He did not mention that the driver had told him to avoid the place and to walk to the village for supplies. "So I went there and marched into it and I said, 'Who is in charge here?' I said it in a very loud voice so that they could not ignore me," he added.

"And what happened?" asked Ned, wide-eyed.

"A huge man, almost seven feet tall, broad-shouldered and most ill-favored, came very close to me so that I could see how large he was and said very gruffly, 'And who wants to know, laddie?'"

Michael was the best of storytellers, and Clarissa had always told him that he should go on the stage. Even the dullest event, when related by Michael, quivered with drama.

Jenny shuddered at his description of the scene. "And what did you say, Michael?"

With a deep bow to his admiring audience, Michael continued. "I, of course, drew myself up to my full height"—and here he showed them precisely how he had done it—"and said, 'I, Michael Delacroix, wish to know, sir. Pray do me the honor of answering my question.'"

"What did he say?" demanded Ned, who had even forgotten to chew as he listened to the story.

Michael grinned down at his little brother. "I believe that he was about to say something very impolite, but then someone sitting in the corner of the room laughed and said, 'Where are your manners, Bart? Answer the gentleman.'"

"The gentleman?" said Clarissa incredulously. "Was he talking about you, Michael?"

Being in his most theatrical mood, he again swept her a low bow. "But of course, dear Claire. How could you doubt it?"

"Then what happened?" asked Ned, who was eating once more and had already disposed of his drumstick and most of his potato. "Did he answer you?"

Michael nodded. "Then the towering oaf, who could have squashed me under his foot, said in a very sulky voice, 'I am in charge.' And then the man in the corner said, urging him on, 'And then, Bart, you must ask how you may be of service to him.'"

"But weren't you afraid of the big man?" asked Jennifer, moving closer to him for comfort.

"I was terrified," he assured her, tucking his arm around her. "I could have happily fainted dead away. But I couldn't let my fear show, little sister, or he most certainly *would* have squashed me—he would have done so at any rate if it hadn't been for the other man. Fortunately, the oaf obeyed him, so when he asked how he could be of service, I told him I needed supper enough for five people."

"And he brought it to you, just like that?" inquired Isobel dryly. "Even though you couldn't pay him?"

"Well, he did look as though he thought he should be paid," admitted Michael, his eyes still bright, "but the other man told him that he would pay for it himself, just to bring me what I asked for."

Isobel stared at him. "But why would a stranger pay for your food?"

"He said that he quite liked my manner, Belle, and that he would give me an errand or two to run for him in order to repay him."

"What sort of errand?" she asked, instantly suspicious.

Michael shrugged. "He didn't say. I daresay he only did me a kindness and when I go back tomorrow, I shall probably have to do something inglorious like blacking his boots for him—or perhaps, if I am fortunate, I shall have something more interesting, like carrying a letter to his ladylove."

"What sort of man is he?" Isobel asked, still wary.

Again her brother shrugged. "His manner and his appearance are those of a gentleman, even though the inn is a rough enough place."

Isobel was forced to be content with that, for the others had finished eating and were already starting to drift off to sleep. She carefully wrapped the remnants of the feast and placed the food high on the stone mantel, where she hoped it would be safe from hungry mice—and from any other four-footed creatures that might come shopping during the night. Then she banked the embers so that the fire would not die out before morning and stood looking down at the younger ones where they lay snuggled together like puppies. She covered them with a blanket, trying not to notice how thin they had gotten during the past weeks. Finally, she wrapped herself in a blanket and lay down next to them.

Michael, she saw approvingly, had pulled his cloak around him and lay stretched across the open doorway, the wooden door having long since rotted away. She was glad to see that he was settling down to sleep, for he had grown as thin as the rest of them, and dark shadows had appeared under his eyes. It was comforting, too, to know that no one could enter the cottage without awakening him. Michael was not always dependable, but he was never lacking in courage. No intruder could enter with Michael stationed there.

As the oldest one, she had borne the burden of worry on their journey. They had been gone for weeks, and the strain was taking a physical and emotional toll on all of them. Now that everyone was asleep and she did not have to act as though their problems would soon be solved, she could feel tears beginning to gather behind her eyelids. Resolutely she brushed them away and forced herself to concentrate on the present. They had one another.

It was not long before she too fell into a deep slumber, comforted that they were all together once more and that there was at least food enough for breakfast. She would worry about tomorrow's other problems when the dawn came.

She was not certain just what awakened her, but she found herself sitting bolt upright, her eyes wide open. The cottage was filled with the cold white light of a spring moon, flooding through the doorway and the gaping hole in the cottage roof. Then she looked again toward the doorway.

Michael was no longer there, but his pack was, and something lay upon it, glistening in the moonlight. Slowly Isobel rose and went over to it, picking it up reluctantly. It was a golden guinea.

How on earth, she wondered, had Michael acquired that much money, and why had he so obviously left it where they would see it?

She stood in the doorway, looking anxiously across the gardens and the fields for any sign of her brother. As she had feared, all was perfectly still.

He had disappeared once more.

CHAPTER 3

Alexandra Lytton leaned against the leather squabs of the carriage, enjoying the unaccustomed luxury of a well-sprung carriage and a team of four. They had stopped at a coaching inn for dinner and a change of horses, and Alexandra had been struck once more by the excellence of the service she received once people saw the Treemore coat of arms on the carriage doors. She was invariably shown immediately to a private dining room and waited upon with the greatest of care. Occasionally she felt that she should ask for something outlandishly difficult for the innkeeper to obtain—like roast larks encased in pastry—just to see if he would be able to manage it.

All in all, her journey had been quite a far cry from her normal humble existence as a governess.

Alicia Treemore had been Alexandra's first charge, and she had been Alicia's governess until three years ago. She had been touched when Alicia had requested Alexandra's company for her wedding. She was fortunate, she knew, for not all governesses were so kindly treated. Alicia had insisted upon sending one of her father's carriages for Alexandra, and she had been treated as an honored guest at the family home in London during the wedding festivities.

It had been a pleasant visit, but a little disconcerting from time to time. Being a governess at so many formal affairs, all of them attended in droves by the cream of Society, had served to remind her sharply of the no-man's-land in which governesses lived—they were neither members of the *ton,* nor were they servants. In appearance and manner they were ladies and mingled with company when invited to do so, but they had none of the status of a lady. Although she was invariably treated politely by the Treemores and their guests, much of the time she had felt that she was invisible to those about her, who were occupied with their own kind. The long ago evening when she had danced with the young eagle had been an interesting exception—but then, of course, he hadn't known that she was a governess. On the whole, putting London behind her once more had been a relief. Alexandra was pleased to be returning home.

She smiled at her choice of words. She no longer had any family of her own, and, for the moment, "home" was a modest lodging for respectable gentlewomen in Torquay. Her last charges, two harum-scarum young boys of ten and eleven, had been successfully prepared for Eton. She now had a two-month holiday of her own before going to her next post, and she was looking forward to reading, relaxing, and walking by the sea. For two months, she would have no demands on her time and no responsibility to serve anyone's needs except her own.

Although they had made a late start from London that morning, the coachman had made good time that day, and they would arrive in Torquay by the next evening. Night had fallen some time earlier, and so the coachman had slowed their pace accordingly. Alexandra was certain that they could not be far from the next coaching inn, where they would stop for the night. She was looking forward to that moment eagerly, not so much because she was either hungry or tired, but because boredom had begun to take its toll. She did not care to light the reading lamp, so she had put away her book and writing desk and had transferred her attention to the passing countryside. However, although the moonlight was bright, looking at a landscape robbed of all color soon lost its charm.

When they rolled to a stop, she looked out hopefully, but she could see that they had only stopped at a tollgate. The keeper, equipped with a lantern, emerged slowly from the small tollhouse beside the gate, and Alexandra could hear the coachman grumbling about his lack of speed.

"I'm like to be an old man before you get here!" he called to the gatekeeper.

"Looks like you're an old 'un already," was the response.

As she sat back from the window, a movement on the other side of the coach caught her eye, and she saw two figures emerge from the shadows of the trees that edged the road there. Then, to her amazement, she heard the words that she had read only in travelers' tales and romances. Most certainly she had never expected to hear them herself in real life.

"Stand and deliver!" said one of the two men who had stepped from the woods.

The speaker's voice was well modulated and, she thought with interest, possibly well educated as well. In the moonlight, she could see the two figures, both tall, though she could not distinguish their build. The speaker's face could not be seen, for he wore a deep-brimmed hat that kept his features shadowed. The other man, wrapped in a dark cloak, stood just behind him. His hat had a shallower brim, but he wore a kerchief tied to hide all of his face save his eyes.

"Hell and damnation!" The driver's box creaked as the heavy coachman wheeled from the gatekeeper toward the highwaymen, and Alexandra could hear the anger in his voice at being taken unawares. The only other person accompanying them was a footman, and a quick glance out the other window showed that the gatekeeper had a pistol trained on him.

The carriage door opened, and the highwayman who had spoken bowed low to her. "If you'll do me the honor of stepping down, ma'am, this will take but an instant of your time."

"The devil it will! You stay just where you are, Miss Lytton!" exclaimed the irate coachman.

"It's perfectly all right," said Alexandra quickly, anxious to avoid any unnecessary confrontation. She rose from the seat and the highwayman took her arm and helped her from the carriage. She had hoped to gain a closer look at his face, but the shadows were thick and he kept his hat pulled low. "I am afraid, though, that you have gone to a great deal of bother for nothing," she told him frankly.

"Certainly you underestimate yourself, ma'am," he assured her. He gestured lightly toward the carriage door and the coat of arms. "After all, that is scarcely the equipage of a poverty-stricken lady."

"Yes, but I am not a member of the family that owns it, sir. I am only a governess who once worked for that family, being returned home to my lodging through the kindness of my former employer. So you see, sir," she told him, leaning forward slightly as she tried to see his expression, "you have put yourself to a deal of trouble for only a handful of servants and our bits of baggage."

She handed him her reticule. "You will see that I speak only the truth. What I have there would not keep you for a week, and I assure you that the jewelry in my box consists of nothing but trumpery pieces, even though I am very fond of them."

He handed the reticule to the man beside him. "Take a look inside it," he said brusquely.

The other man glanced at Alexandra, paused a moment as though he were hesitant, then pulled the drawstring and tumbled the reticule's contents into his open palm.

The speaker had been studying her as she stood in the patch of moonlight where he had placed her, but he now took a quick glance at the coins and handkerchief and small tortoiseshell comb his companion was holding.

"I see that you were telling no more than the truth, ma'am," he said, nodding at her possessions. "I think, though, that I must be certain. As you say, I have gone to considerable trouble, so I'll just have a look in the things you're carrying up top."

"That you will not!" This was too much for the indignant coachman, who half rose from his perch with the whip in his hand, ignoring the shouted warning of the footman.

To Alexandra's horror, the highwayman who had been speaking raised a pistol and aimed it at the coachman. Just as he did so, the man who had opened her reticule flung himself forward, knocking the shooter's arm to one side just as he fired.

"No!" exclaimed the man who had thus interfered. "You said there'd be no one hurt!"

Alexandra heard an exclamation of pain just after the shot was fired, and the coachman fell back upon his box. Almost immediately another shot rang out, and the man in the kerchief sank to the ground. The gatekeeper, having shifted his attention to the coachman, had been edging his way around the front of the coach, so the footman had taken his opportunity and fired his own pistol. His aim had been more accurate than that of the highwayman.

"Nor would there have been anyone hurt, you poor fool!" exclaimed the highwayman, looking down at his companion and prodding him with his boot. The man on the ground groaned but made no other response.

In the distance Alexandra heard the welcome rumbling of wheels and she realized with gratitude that someone else was approaching the tollgate. The highwayman and gate-keeper seemed to melt into the trees at the edge of the road as the footman scrambled to the ground, the coachman following him somewhat more slowly.

"Are you all right then, Miss Lytton?" asked Davis, the burly coachman, looking down at her in concern. He had no desire to report a disaster such as an injured passenger to his master.

"Yes, I'm perfectly fine," she replied. "But what of you, Davis? You've been wounded." She could see a stain of something dark across his forehead when he removed his hat.

He pulled out a large handkerchief and wiped the blood from his brow. "The shot only grazed me, ma'am. No harm done."

Satisfied that what he said was true, she bent over the highwayman who had been shot and removed the kerchief from his face. It was just as she had thought as she had listened to his voice and watched his movements.

"He's nothing but a boy," she told the other two, who did not look impressed by the news.

The coachman snorted. "That won't be saving him, ma'am. It's best for him if he dies. If James hadn't shot him, the hangman would have him."

Alexandra looked up at him. "But if this boy hadn't interfered, Davis, you might well be dead instead of having suffered only a mild injury."

The coachman shifted his weight uneasily. This was an aspect of the situation that he had not considered. "Still, Miss Lytton," he protested, "surely you're not taking his part. James shot him after they had fired at us."

Alexandra turned back the dark cloak and opened the boy's jacket. A dark strain was spreading across the front of his white shirt. With a sharp exclamation, she turned to the coachman and motioned toward the carriage.

"Hand me my bandbox, Davis! I'll not have this boy bleeding to death while we stand idly by and watch it happen!"

"Get it then, James!" he said sharply. He had no desire to have the death of a boy on his head, highwayman or not.

Whether the coachman felt a twinge of remorse or whether he was merely accustomed to following orders wasn't clear to Alexandra, but she had no time to think of it just then, for the boy's blood was flowing far too freely. She opened the bandbox and pulled out a chemise made of fine linen, folded it into a pad, and pressed it over the wound, holding it firmly in place with the heel of her hand.

By this time a cart had pulled up behind them and its driver, a young farmer, had joined them and stood looking down at Alexandra and the boy.

"What's happened here then?" asked the farmer. "How came the boy to be shot?"

"He's a robbing thief!" said the footman, who was collecting Alexandra's reticule and its scattered contents.

"What?" the farmer asked in amazement. "This boy, alone and on foot, robbed you? He attacked the two of you in this carriage? Where's his gun?"

"There were three of them, and the other two were armed!" returned the coachman defensively, flushing at the farmer's tone. "One of the rogues was the gatekeeper."

"The gatekeeper?" demanded the farmer. "John Olsen wouldn't take a penny that didn't belong to him, for all he keeps a tollgate. He fell on hard times and lost his patch of land, or he'd never be working this job."

Before anyone could respond to this, he strode to the tollhouse, shouting for Olsen. After a few minutes he returned, escorting a frail old man who looked badly shaken.

"Found him tied up in there," said the farmer grimly. "Trussed like a fowl for the spit."

"Do you know this boy?" asked Alexandra, still on her knees beside him, holding the linen pad in place.

The old gatekeeper stooped close to him and stared at his face, then shook his head slowly. "Don't belong hereabouts."

"Olsen said that he didn't recognize the man who tied him up either, but I'd wager that they'd recognize both of them at The Bull and Basket! That's a place for rogues and thieves if ever there was one!" said the farmer grimly.

"At the moment," interrupted Alexandra, "our main concern is to get this boy to a bed and send for a surgeon. Where is the closest place we can take him?"

"Should be reporting him to the nearest magistrate," grumbled the coachman, but a look from her silenced him.

"There's a proper inn, The Gray Goose, just a mile beyond the gate," replied the farmer, "and they can send for a surgeon from there. An ostler can go faster on horseback than I can go for him in my cart."

"Then that's what we will do," said Alexandra briskly. "Now, sir," she said, looking up at the farmer, "if you will be so kind as to help us move this boy into the carriage, we shall be on our way."

Soon the boy was stretched on the leather seat of the carriage, Alexandra still kneeling beside him with the chemise folded firmly in place, although she could see that it was growing steadily more blood-soaked and soon would do no good. The carriage proceeded slowly down the road, the coachman having been cautioned not to bounce them about.

When they reached The Gray Goose, things moved swiftly. A boy was dispensed hastily for Mr. Jameson, the local surgeon, and the innkeeper helped them to settle the boy in a bed and sent his wife to find cloth suitable for bandages. He had at first shown some reluctance when he knew the nature of the wound and was told that the boy had been involved in an attempted robbery, but Alexandra had made short work of that. She was both ladylike and authoritative in manner, and the innkeeper, as he told his protesting wife later, recognized a member of the quality when he saw one. And then, of course, there was the carriage with the Treemore coat of arms, which was equally impressive.

By the time Mr. Jameson had completed his ministrations, the boy was breathing more easily, although he had still not regained consciousness, nor had his color returned.

"Since it's a clean shoulder wound, he'll mend quickly," he told Alexandra as he washed and dried his hands and rolled down his shirtsleeves. "But he wouldn't have fared so well if you'd left him to bleed, miss." She had provided him with a clear account of the evening's events as he had worked.

He watched her for a moment. "What are you going to do with him now?" he asked.

She shook her head. "I wish that I knew. I am certain that I won't have him turned over to a magistrate, but no one seems to know who he is, so I can't turn him over to his family, and I can't very well leave him here."

"You're taking a very great deal of trouble with him, Miss Lytton," he observed, his shrewd eyes still regarding her closely. "Most would say that he brought this trouble upon his own head."

She smiled at Mr. Jameson. "He would not be the first young boy to do something ill-advised. I think this injury is probably a heavy enough payment for his lack of judgment."

"Robbing someone at gunpoint is scarcely merely ill-advised, ma'am," observed the surgeon dryly. "He may go back out and do the same thing as soon as he's able."

"I don't believe he will. He had no gun and he didn't want one used. If it hadn't been for him, the coachman would have been lying on the road."

The surgeon shrugged on his coat and turned back to speak to her at the door of the chamber. "I got him to swallow a little laudanum, so he'll sleep the night through and I'll be round to see to him tomorrow."

"You've been very kind, Mr. Jameson. Thank you for coming."

The surgeon nodded and closed the door behind him. Alexandra sat for a while, studying the quiet face on the pillow.

Just what *was* she going to do? she asked herself. She could scarcely take him back to her lodging in Torquay, and she could not detain the Treemore carriage and servants. After all, they were expected back in London at an appointed time.

What she needed was the young man's identity so that he could be returned to his family and cared for properly—and so that she could inform his parents of their son's evening activities. Just how she was going to do that was another question.

As she carefully recalled the events of the evening, however, the answer came to her clearly. Although she did not relish the visit, she would undertake it.

The next morning she would go to The Bull and Basket. Doubtless someone there would be able to identify him.

CHAPTER 4

The next morning Alexandra checked on the patient and found him still sleeping, although he was flushed and feverish and tossed restlessly on his pillow. She soaked a cloth in cool water and washed his face with it, wondering uneasily when Mr. Jameson would arrive. After watching out the window for a few minutes, she went down to ask the landlord the location of The Bull and Basket. At least, she thought, she could be doing something constructive.

"The Bull and Basket?" the landlord repeated blankly. "Forgive me, miss, but why would a lady like yourself be interested in that den of thieves?"

Alexandra, who had been prepared for such a reaction because of the young farmer's description of the place, answered him calmly. "I believe that someone there might know who this boy is."

He shook his head violently—or at least as violently as a small, very round man could manage. "If the boy's a member of that crew, I don't want him under my roof, and that's the truth! Nor do you want anything to do with him, miss! There's no telling but what they might take it into their heads to come and get him!"

Alexandra had not thought of this possibility, but she smiled reassuringly, ignoring the fact that the landlord's plump hands were beginning to tremble convulsively.

"But you've seen the boy yourself. You can tell at a glance that he's no ruffian."

"That's as may be," he replied. "But word has it that at least one of them at The Bull and Basket is a gentlemen of sorts—or was before he become a gentleman of the highway. That lad must belong to him."

Alexandra had not thought of this, either, and the possibility shook her. She remembered now that she had noticed the highwayman's polished manner and speech, but she had not connected that observation to the boy. Still, by no means would she wish to leave him at The Bull and Basket, father or no father. Almost immediately, however, another thought reassured her.

"Surely you don't think that a father would leave his own son lying on the roadside, Mr. Springfield," she replied crisply.

The landlord shook his head slowly, ruffling his dark hair as he thought the matter over so that it stood in spikes, giving him a very alert appearance. "Who's to say what a scoundrel mightn't do? A decent man wouldn't leave his own flesh and blood behind, but then Gentleman Jack is no decent man."

"Gentleman Jack? Do you mean that you know the name of the man who attempted to rob us last night?" Her voice was sharp and the landlord moved uncomfortably. The words had come without his consent, for he had no wish to grow involved in the matter. Every instinct of self-preservation militated against it.

"I don't know it for a certainty," he protested. "He mightn't be the same man at all!"

"But you suspect that he is," she pressed, determined to have as much information as she could wrest from him.

The landlord nodded reluctantly. "I've never clapped eyes on him myself, but last autumn there were stories about a highwayman calling himself Gentleman Jack. He operated near another tollgate over by Shellingham but, like I said, that was last autumn."

"But you think that the man last night was this Gentleman Jack because he tried to rob us at a tollgate?"

"Don't you say another word, Reggie!" His wife, a tiny woman with fierce black eyes, appeared behind him. "You'll bring trouble on our heads, sure as life!"

"Talking to me will certainly not cause trouble for you, Mrs. Springfield." Alexandra tried to be as firm and reassuring as possible in her manner. "Your husband has said nothing that would create a problem for you!"

"Indeed?" Mrs. Springfield clearly did not believe a word of it. "Just talking about such things can bring trouble, miss."

Alexandra considered Mrs. Springfield's unyielding expression and her husband's nervous one for a moment. "I need to know how to get to The Bull and Basket," she replied. "I mean to have my coachman drive me there this morning." Her voice and her manner were stiff, and she hoped that a reminder of the carriage and its coat of arms would have some effect.

To her relief, she saw that, although Mrs. Springfield maintained her stony expression, her husband was beginning to give way once more.

"You won't tell anyone that I gave you directions, miss?" His eyes and voice were pleading, and he tried to ignore his wife's sniff of disapproval. "Nor mention that you and the boy are staying here at The Gray Goose?"

"Naturally I will not," replied Alexandra, sounding a great deal more assured than she felt. She was grateful that she would be accompanied by the sturdy coachman and footman, and she hoped devoutly that they would see no one at The Bull and Basket that they recognized. She had already created more trouble for the Treemore servants than she had intended by insisting on bringing the boy with them. All she wanted now was a little information.

She waited anxiously until Mr. Jameson appeared and checked on the patient. He frowned as he removed the bandage and inspected the wound, which had grown angry-looking.

"Infection," he said briefly, and turned to rummage in his bag. Alexandra turned away as he began to clean the wound, trying not to hear the boy's moans. After a few minutes, he had a fresh poultice in place and had dosed the patient with laudanum once more.

"More rest will do him good," the surgeon told her. "But you can see for yourself that this has been a setback."

Alexandra nodded. "But it's only a temporary one, isn't it?"

Mr. Jameson shrugged. "More than likely. He's young—but he's not much more than skin and bones. I'd say he hasn't been eating regularly for quite a while."

She could see for herself that this was true, and she wondered once more about where he belonged. Perhaps he was one of those unhappy youngsters who had no home. He had struck her as being gently bred, though, and his clothes, although threadbare, were of good quality.

Alexandra sighed. Perhaps he had no family to find.

As though he had read her mind, the surgeon inquired, "Have you decided what you will do with him when you leave today, Miss Lytton?"

She nodded, trying to regain some of the hope she had felt earlier. "I hope to locate his family this morning."

"Indeed?" His bushy eyebrows rose abruptly at this. "And how do you propose to do that?"

She forced herself to remain completely composed, and not by so much as the blink of an eyelash did she betray her misgivings. "I shall have my coachman drive me to The Bull and Basket so that I may discover if anyone there knows his identity."

If Mr. Jameson's eyebrows could have disappeared completely from his forehead, they would have done so. "The Bull and Basket! I suppose that idiot Springfield told you about that nest of ne'er-do-wells!"

Alexandra shook her head. "The farmer who helped us last night mentioned it and indicated that he thought the robbers might be known there. Mr. Springfield has done his best to convince me not to go."

"Then he's got more wit than I've credited him with, which is more than I can say for you, young lady!" Mr. Jameson regarded her ferociously from under his gray brows. "I had thought you a sensible woman, if somewhat misguided, but I must withdraw that opinion! You stand here and tell me that, even though you know that you will be waltzing into a place that harbors all the unsavory characters in the countryside, you still plan to go!" He shook his head in disbelief.

"Have you a better suggestion?" she asked. "When I helped that boy, I accepted at least some responsibility for his welfare, and I must make an effort to help him."

"You have already done so," he said brusquely. "You kept him from dying on the road and you paid my fee. You put him in a decent bed so that he could sleep, and you didn't turn him over to the magistrate. You've done more than most would have bothered to do."

"And now you suggest that I walk away and leave him for the innkeeper to turn out onto the road?" she demanded. "At least if I go to The Bull and Basket, I may discover the whereabouts of his family."

The more she had thought about the boy's behavior with Gentleman Jack last night—if the highwayman had indeed been Gentleman Jack—the more convinced she had become that their relationship was not that of father and son. She felt the force of Mr. Jameson's argument, but she could not see any other hope of identifying the boy.

Indeed, seeing him now, she had almost decided that if the trip to The Bull and Basket bore no fruit, she would send the coach back to London and remain here herself until he had recovered. If he had a family, he could tell her who they were when he regained consciousness and she could see him restored to them. If he had none, then she would do what she could to help him along his way. In either case, she would be able to live with her conscience.

Mr. Jameson shook his head. "I can see there's no reasoning with you, Miss Lytton."

"Indeed there's not, sir," she responded, smiling to take the edge off her words. "But I do appreciate your warning me and I shall see you when you come again to tend your patient. Perhaps I shall have news for you then."

He looked at her in surprise. "I thought that you would be going on your way. Will you still be here this evening?"

"Yes. I cannot go when he is doing so poorly."

He was still shaking his head as he went down the stairs to his gig. As he started away from the inn, he looked up to where she stood at the window, and touched his whip to the brim of his hat in salute.

Alexandra felt far from confident as she got into the Treemore coach and they started on their way. She had explained the situation to both of the servants, and they were too well trained to allow their dismay to show. She could feel the ripples of disapproval, however.

As they drew close to The Bull and Basket, she began to fear that she had made an error and was putting the two men in danger. The road was little frequented and full of potholes, so Davis drove slowly and carefully.

James, his pistol close at hand, kept a wary eye on every tree they passed. The inn itself was as unprepossessing as she had expected it to be, but when the coach came to a stop and James opened the door for her, she stepped down brightly.

"I shall not be long," she said, tucking into her reticule the sketch she had made of the boy that morning. At least, she thought, she would not have to rely upon a verbal description. Showing the picture should be helpful.

"I will come with you, Miss Lytton, while Davis watches the carriage," said James.

"Nonsense!" she said briskly. She had no intention of having either Davis or James come inside the inn. She did not for a moment believe that its inmates would harm a young woman with a coach waiting for her just outside. And she certainly had no intention of endangering either servant any more than she already had.

She walked in as James held the door for her, and her glance sent him reluctantly back to the carriage to wait with the coachman.

The exterior of the inn was not attractive, but she was surprised and pleased to see that the taproom tables had been recently scrubbed and that there was a fire. A small barmaid in a white cap peered at her cautiously from a corner of the room.

Alexandra smiled at her and removed the sketch from her reticule. "Could you tell me if you know this boy?" she asked, showing it to the girl.

She looked at it with no sign of recognition and shook her head.

"Is there anyone else here?" Alexandra asked, disappointed. "Could I perhaps see the landlord?"

The girl disappeared through a door leading to a passage, and Alexandra glanced about her. Even though the girl had not recognized him, nothing that had happened in the inn thus far was anything but ordinary. She had certainly not been set upon by thieves. Perhaps the visit would not be so unpleasant after all.

She had scarcely allowed herself the thought when the largest man she had ever seen entered the room, the barmaid following in his wake. If the inn had looked unprepossessing, it had perhaps modeled itself after its owner.

"What do you want then?" he demanded, his voice rough. He nodded toward the barmaid, who had scuttled back to her corner. "She said you had a picture and was asking questions."

Calmly, Alexandra had handed him the sketch. "Yes. I asked her if she knew this boy."

He snatched it from her hand, gave it a quick glance, and tore it two. Striding over to the fire, he tossed it in.

"Do you know who he is?" Alexandra asked evenly, determined not to appear intimidated by his behavior.

"No, I don't! No more do I know what you're doing here, nosing around where you have no business!"

"Really, Bart! Your manners are deplorable." The speaker had entered the room quietly, just in time for this interchange.

Alexandra turned sharply at the sound of his voice. "You!"

He bowed. "Yes, Miss Lytton, it is I. And I must apologize for the boorish behavior of the landlord. He is not accustomed to serving ladies."

"But apparently he *is* in the habit of giving space in his inn to highwaymen!" she responded tartly.

He shook his head reproachfully. "Really, Miss Lytton, you are too hard upon him. I have stopped here only a few days and am now on my way so that I do not create any awkwardness for Bart and his establishment."

"Where is the family of the boy that was with you last night?" she asked. She did not believe that he was the boy's father. The man before her was fair in coloring, his features gently modeled rather than finely chiseled like the boy's. Nothing in face or body proclaimed their relationship.

He shook his head regretfully. "I cannot tell you. I had just met the lad. I needed a little help with last night's undertaking, and I could see that he was in need of some assistance himself. We were able to be of some service to one another."

"You didn't even learn his name?"

"Well, I do know that," he conceded. "He introduced himself to Bart as Michael Delacroix—and I might add that he did so in such a manner as to make me take an interest in him. It's a thousand pities that he got himself shot."

Alexandra stiffened at this cavalier mention of the shooting. "Michael Delacroix," she said, thinking it over. "But you know nothing of his family?"

"All that I know of him is that he traded supper and a guinea for assisting me last night."

"Supper for five it was," said Bart sourly. "He took enough for a small army."

"So it was," agreed the highwayman. "How very astute of you to remember, Bart."

"Fair cleaned out my kitchen, he did," complained the landlord.

"Ah, yes, but you must recall that I paid you for his supper, Bart," the highwayman reminded him gently. "In fact, I paid you very well indeed."

Before Alexandra could inquire into the interesting matter of supper for five, someone else spoke.

"Excuse me, sir. We are looking for our brother, Michael Delacroix, and we thought he might find him here."

In the doorway stood Isobel, flanked by Clarissa, Ned, and Jennifer.

The highwayman turned to Alexandra and bowed. "Miss Lytton, I am happy to see that your question has been answered. And now, though I regret depriving myself of such charming company, I believe that I must take my leave."

He glanced toward the front of the inn. "And because I have no wish to inconvenience your servants, ma'am, I shall make my departure quietly through the kitchen door. I should hate to disturb them."

Here he turned to Bart. "I shall trouble you no more, my friend. Should the Bow Street Runners inquire after me, you may say with honesty that you have no notion of my destination."

Tipping his hat to the room at large, he slipped through the doorway and departed.

Turning back to the children once more, Alexandra smiled. "I have been looking for you," she told them. "If you will come with me, I will take you to Michael."

CHAPTER 5

Pamela looked approvingly at the new curricle, drawn by two perfectly matched bays, as the groom pulled up smartly to the front of Greengage Manor.

"How splendid, Richard!" She turned and rewarded him with a smile. "I didn't know that you kept a curricle here, too!" She had thoroughly enjoyed being driven about London in his very stylish equipage, the object of envying glances from less fortunate young women obliged to walk the pavements.

"I think that you should have a phaeton for country driving," he said, helping her into the equipage and then leaping lightly in beside her. "It would make living here more pleasant for you, and I believe you would enjoy it."

"I am certain that I should like it above all things." She dismissed from her mind the reference to living in the country. The phaeton would be delightful, and she would need one for town driving, too—preferably a high-perch phaeton, which was considered particularly dashing.

She paused to wave to her mother, who had come out to see them off. She and Richard were going to pay an afternoon call on Mrs. Pendergrass. Mrs. Wingate had planned to go with them, but she was recovering from a headache and had decided that bouncing about in country lanes might invite its return.

"Enjoy yourself, children," she called after them. "And do explain to dear Mrs. Pendergrass why I am not with you."

Pamela waved again and then sat back to enjoy herself as the curricle went bowling down the drive. If her mother had not developed a headache, they would have been obliged to take a stodgy carriage, since the curricle could carry only two. It was, she thought, singularly fortunate that, if her mother must have a headache, she should have had one in such a timely manner. Riding in the elegant little curricle almost offset the gloomy knowledge that they were going to call on Mrs. Pendergrass—who she knew beyond a shadow of doubt would bore her to tears.

All of their dinner guests had come to call upon them the following day, and Pamela and Richard had been conscientiously returning their calls. He was anxious for Pamela to become more closely acquainted with all of them and to feel at home, and she was anxious for the others to be impressed by her manners and her style.

Her spirits had been somewhat dashed by the discovery that few of their dinner party guests were young and fashionable. Nonetheless, she recognized that several of them were people of consequence. As long as they were making admiring remarks to her and about her, Pamela found Richard's neighbors charming. When the subject changed, however, she noticed that the conversation grew unbearably tedious.

"Do you suppose Mrs. Pendergrass will tell us more stories about her husband?" The question was rhetorical. She was certain that Mrs. Pendergrass would do precisely that.

"I suppose she will, but you must be indulgent, my dear. She wants you to know all about him because she likes you and because she was—"

"Yes, I know, Richard," she interrupted, "and she was

so *very* fond of your grandmother that she is almost like family."

"I didn't realize that I had been boring you by repeating myself." His response was a little stiff, and his eyes remained fixed on the road.

"Oh, Richard," she said swiftly, putting her hand on his knee, "of course you're not boring me! *You* could never do that! It's just that—well, that I feel so uncomfortable when I am with her. I don't believe she really likes me."

This did draw his gaze and he looked at her in astonishment. "Not like you? How foolish you are being, Pamela! She thinks you are quite wonderful!"

Pamela gave her head a tiny shake. "No, she really doesn't, Richard. I can tell by the way she looks at me."

Richard laughed. "Pamela, you are imagining things! You are simply letting your nerves get the better of you."

Pamela, who hadn't a nerve in her body, allowed her voice to quiver slightly. "Do you really think so, Richard?"

He nodded his head emphatically. "You have been unfailingly gracious since your arrival. She thinks that you are splendid."

Their call went precisely as Pamela had expected it to. Mrs. Pendergrass served them tea and dry biscuits and told them at least five stories about Melvin Pendergrass, her late husband.

"Dear Deidre was so fond of Melvin, and we were equally attached to her," she said, looking at Browning with a softened expression. "And you are so *very* much like your grandmother."

"You see," Pamela remarked on the drive home. "I told you that she doesn't like me."

Browning glanced at her, puzzled. "I didn't see her do or say anything that should make you think such a thing, Pamela."

His fiancée pouted prettily. "You heard her, Richard. She was talking about your grandmother again and about how much like her you are. She *adores* you."

"And I'm very fond of her," he replied, smiling. "She has always been kind to me."

He paused and glanced at Pamela once more, a little puzzled by her conviction of Mrs. Pendergrass's dislike of her. "That has nothing to do with not liking you, however."

Pamela shrugged one dainty shoulder. "All of her conversation is about the past—except when she talks about you. She has no time for anything or anyone else."

Mystified, he sank into a troubled silence.

After a few moments, Pamela allowed her lip to tremble and turned to him. "Richard, I am so *desperately* unhappy here! Are all of your friends here *old?*"

Browning laughed. "You know that not all of my friends are old, Pamela! Why, Matt and Clara Damson are certainly not antiques! And you've met Jack Bartholomew and Freddie Taverner and—"

"I don't mean your friends in town, Richard. I am referring to your friends *here!* And have you listened to the Damsons' conversation? Why, it is enough to put me to sleep! They may not seem old to you, but they most certainly do to me!"

He paused, struck by the truth of her tactless comment. "I had not thought of it, Pamela," he said slowly, "but, honestly, not everyone here is old. You met Tom Merriweather at the dinner party and—"

"Yes, but, other than the Damsons and us, he was the only there who didn't need a cane!"

"You must remember, Pamela, that some of the younger members of their families, like Lady Trillby's son and daughter and their children, are in London now for the Season. You remember meeting them there."

Pamela nodded her head impatiently. "Yes, they are sensible people. They live in town rather than out here, where nothing exciting ever happens!"

Browning cursed himself silently for not having anticipated her need for younger company. What he said was true, and some of the members of local society *were* in town, but he was suddenly painfully aware that Pamela would undoubtedly consider the men of his own age— most of whom were settled with families—as standing in imminent need of the cane she had mentioned.

As they rounded a turn in the road, he caught a glimpse of the frothy orchards and felt his heart lift as it always did. Certainly, he thought, when Pamela focused upon that vision of loveliness, she would grow less troubled by their call and think of more pleasant things. After all, life here had much to offer.

As she looked at Greengage Manor, her thoughts took quite a different turn, however.

"I do not think that we should stay here a day longer," she announced suddenly. "Marie Ridley's ball is to be held next week, and I still need to have a final fitting for my gown. And we have our own ball to prepare for as well. I cannot think why we should stay here, buried in the country, when we have so much to do."

Browning frowned a little. He had promised that their trip would be a short one, but they had scarcely arrived. He knew that they had many engagements in London, but they suddenly held little appeal for him. Greengage had woven its usual spell around him, and he was reluctant to leave. And he still clung to the hope that she too would fall in love with the place. Thinking of this, he had a sudden inspiration.

"Would you like to go on a picnic this afternoon, Pamela?" he asked.

She turned to stare at him. "A picnic? Why ever would we do that?"

"Just to go down to the orchards and spend some time there. We could have Mrs. Melling pack us a light supper. Your mother is invited too, of course, if she's feeling well enough."

Pamela's expression grew mulish. "Richard, I think that we should have dinner *inside* in the dining room, just as we normally do. And, at any rate, I need to talk to Mrs. Melling."

Browning glanced at her warily. "What do you need to discuss with Mrs. Melling, Pamela?"

"I need to talk give her instructions about the house party, and I thought that I would also have a talk with her about what my expectations will be when I am mistress here," she replied. "It is fortunate that we made this trip to the country, for it will help me to begin to organize the household."

There was a brief silence. Then Browning said gently, "Perhaps you should wait just a little before organizing the household, my dear. After all, you wish to go back to London immediately."

"That's true, of course, Richard, but I think one can never begin too soon in reaching an understanding with one's servants."

After another brief pause, Browning spoke again in a still gentler voice. "But you forget, Pamela, that I have long ago reached an understanding with them."

This time he had her full attention. "Do you mean to say, Richard," she said slowly, "that you do not *wish* for me to be in charge of running the household?"

"I am simply saying that it will be best to go slowly. After all, my dear, they have been accustomed to me for many years, and to my grandmother before that. Most of the servants are not newly come to my service, and they have proven their worth."

"And the house party?" she demanded. "You don't wish for me to instruct them about my wishes for that?"

"Pamela, you have the ball and the wedding to prepare for. Why not leave the house party in their hands and not trouble yourself about it? They have done this countless times."

"I understand perfectly! You want me to allow the servants to do just as they wish to do, and to run roughshod over me as they do over you!"

Browning did not reply for a moment, as he tried unsuccessfully to picture Butterworth and Mrs. Melling running roughshod over him. They had reached the front door of the manor house by this time, and the groom, who had been watching for him, ran out to take the reins and drive the curricle to the stables. Pamela, not waiting for his assistance or that of the footman, hopped nimbly down and hurried to the house.

Richard watched her go, reading himself a lecture as he did so. He knew that she was very young and that dealing with her was going to take a careful hand. He was going to have to think of an arrangement that satisfied Pamela without oversetting Mrs. Melling, Butterworth, and the entire household. Marriage, he reflected, was going to take considerably more effort than he had anticipated.

Suddenly returning to London held a certain appeal. At least there Pamela would be so occupied with a whirl of social activities that she would have little time to spend on rearranging his household. Of course, he admitted to himself, she had already begun to rearrange his life. No doubt he should not have allowed her free rein in planning his days. She had taken the bit and run with it.

Sighing, he straightened his shoulders and strolled inside to pour oil on the troubled waters and to think of a way to regain control of his life without losing his fiancée.

CHAPTER 6

Isobel and the children had looked at Alexandra doubtfully as she led them from The Bull and Basket but, on the other hand, having seen the proprietor of the inn, they were not inclined to linger inside, either. When they realized that they were about to ride in the impressive carriage parked outside the inn, all of them stared in wonder at its glossy doors and the coat of arms painted on them.

"I am Alexandra Lytton," she told them, as James opened the door for her and looked dubiously at the children. Although reasonably clean, they were dressed in worn clothing, some of it so tattered that it would be better described as rags. They certainly did not look as though they belonged in such a vehicle.

"They are coming back with us to The Gray Goose," she said to him, and stood aside so that he could help each of the children into the carriage, where they perched wide-eyed on the very edge of the seats. After James had helped Alexandra in last, Isobel took the introductions in hand.

"I am Isobel Delacroix," she said, sitting up very straight and crossing her ankles in a graceful, ladylike manner that did not escape Alexandra. Given her circumstances, the girl's attempt at propriety was touching.

"And these are my sisters and brother, Clarissa, Jennifer, and Ned."

She indicated each one with a nod, and each of the children in turn nodded politely at Alexandra. They all had the same coloring and the same slender frame as Michael. Alexandra reflected that she would have known that they belonged to the same family without anyone ever mentioning a name.

"Is The Gray Goose an inn?" asked Clarissa, unable to control her anxiety. "Is that where Michael is?"

Alexandra nodded. "Where may I find your parents?" she asked. "Perhaps we should get them before going to Michael."

The children exchanged a quick glance, but it was a moment before Isobel spoke. "Our parents are dead," she replied briefly.

"I am sorry to hear that." Alexandra's response was automatic, but it was sincere as well—for several reasons. She was sorry for the children's loss, sorry for the miserable state in which they had obviously found themselves—and sorry for herself because she now appeared to have five children on her hands rather than one.

All of the children, she knew, were watching her warily, so she chose her next words carefully. "Do you live nearby?" she asked as casually as she could. "I am a stranger here myself, so I don't know the local families."

Isobel, who was clearly the spokesman, shook her head. "No, we don't. We have traveled from some distance."

"Indeed?" Alexandra's tone was interested. "Where are you going?"

They all glanced at one another once more and there was another pause. The silence grew longer until Clarissa could finally bear it no longer.

"Are you really taking us to see Michael?" she demanded. "Why did he not come back to us last night?"

"Yes, I am indeed taking you to him," Alexandra reassured her. Then, looking at Clarissa, she said, "Tell me, please, just where Michael was to come to you. Even though you've come from a distance, you must have had a meeting place."

The other three looked at Clarissa, who in turn looked down at the toes of her worn slippers. She had no desire to tell this well-dressed lady that they had been staying in an abandoned cottage.

"I see," said Alexandra finally. And she was indeed beginning to believe that her worst fears for them were true. Given their physical condition and the state of their clothing, they had been on the road for quite some time, and she was not at all convinced that they had a destination. Sadly, she thought to herself that they must be homeless waifs. Undoubtedly that was the reason their brother Michael had gotten himself into this predicament. He had been trying to provide for them.

They were all watching her intently, so Alexandra took herself in hand and smiled at them as reassuringly as she could.

"I want to prepare you to see Michael," she told them. "He has had an accident, and so—"

"How badly hurt is he?" asked Isobel, her eyes fixed upon Alexandra. Jennifer had begun to cry quietly and both Clarissa and Ned looked shaken.

"I think he will be quite all right," said Alexandra, "and a surgeon is looking after him. When I left the inn, however, he had not regained consciousness because the surgeon had given him some laudanum to help him rest." For the most part, she did not believe in withholding upsetting information from children, who were, she knew, likely to conjure up situations far more dreadful than the truth.

"You see, Jenny, Michael will be all right," Isobel said,

putting her arm around her little sister. "And we are going to see him in just a few minutes."

"Yes, indeed you are. And I know that he will be very glad to see you."

"How was he hurt?" asked Isobel, her throat tight with a fear that she was trying not to show. When he had not appeared this morning, she had been certain that he had somehow gotten into trouble. Now she was doing her best to brace herself. At least, she thought, Miss Lytton appeared to be a responsible, kindly person, so he was being taken care of properly.

Alexandra looked hesitantly at the younger children, wondering for a moment if this might not be too much information for them, but Isobel spoke firmly. "We are a family. We all need to know about Michael."

Alexandra nodded. "I'm afraid that he was shot," she said quietly.

The children froze. Then Clarissa said hoarsely, "Who shot him?"

"My footman," she replied. "Or more correctly, since this is not my carriage, the footman of the Treemore family."

"But why would the footman shoot Michael?" Clarissa demanded. "Was it an accident?"

"No, I'm afraid that it wasn't. Michael was with two highwaymen."

Isobel groaned and covered her eyes. This was exactly the kind of thing that she had feared. Michael was always prone to mischief, and even when he was trying to be helpful, he could not seem to keep from getting himself into the most dangerous situations she could imagine.

"I knew it!" said Clarissa, whose mind had been working along the same lines as her sister's.

Ned was still staring at Alexandra, awe-stricken. "Highwaymen?" He spoke in the same tone that a true believer would use about Mecca. "Real, honest-to-goodness highwaymen?"

Alexandra nodded. "Yes, they were real highwaymen."

"And they tried to rob you as you were traveling in your carriage?" asked Isobel, piecing it together.

"Yes, they did try. However, if it's any comfort to you, your brother was very brave."

"Oh yes, most certainly he was," agreed Isobel, in a voice that said he was anything except brave. "It requires great courage to take a pistol and try to hold up a lady in a coach."

"Actually, Michael had no pistol. The other two did, however. The one standing beside Michael was going to shoot my coachman, but Michael spoiled his aim so that the coachman was only grazed by the bullet."

"And is that when Michael was shot?" asked Clarissa.

"Unfortunately, yes. The footman was merely shooting in the direction of the attackers."

There was a brief silence while they digested this information. Then Isobel, who had been watching Alexandra closely, said slowly, "But you said that Michael is at an inn and that he has had a surgeon. Have you had him taken prisoner?"

Ned and Jennifer, who had not considered such a thing, looked stunned, and Jennifer started to cry once more. Even Ned began to look as though highwaymen were losing some of their charm for him.

Hastily Alexandra leaned over and patted Jennifer's knee consolingly. "Oh no, my dear, indeed I have not had him arrested. I could see that he was only a boy and that he tried to prevent an injury."

At that, Isobel's calm demeanor cracked and she burst into tears, shocking her sisters and brother by this unaccustomed display of emotion. "Oh, thank you, Miss Lytton, thank you!" she managed to sob. "I was so afraid

for him, and I know that you could have had him arrested! If you had, I don't know what we would have
done!"

Alexandra leaned forward and patted her hand reassuringly. "Everything will be quite all right," she told
them all. "You see, here we are at the inn. You shall see
Michael, and have some supper and a bath and a warm
bed to sleep in."

That much at least she could supply for them, she told
herself. Even though she did not carry much money in
her reticule, she did have quite enough for their needs
in her box. She feared what might happen to these children next, but she could make the rest of this day and
the night as comfortable as possible.

To her relief, Michael's eyes were open when they went
to his room, and he was able to recognize his family. He
had just awakened, so everything was still hazy to him.
Alexandra allowed the children to say hello and to see for
themselves that he was not at death's door. Then she ush-
ered them from the room, telling them that Michael was
going to have some hot soup and then needed to rest.

"Come along now and we shall find something for all
of you to eat," said Alexandra cheerfully.

"Do you mean that we get to eat *now?*" asked Ned,
amazed. "We had breakfast today and usually we have
to wait for ever so much longer than this before we eat
again!"

Clarissa stepped sharply on his toe and he looked up
at her indignantly. "Here now, Claire! I wasn't in your
way! Why are you treading on my toes?"

Alexandra ignored Ned's embarrassing observation
about their eating habits, as well as the brief encounter
between him and Clarissa. Turning to Isobel, she said, "I
have engaged these two rooms so that you can be near
Michael. I hope that you won't mind sharing."

"You're very good," said Isobel, flushing. "Of course we won't mind." She didn't add that it had been weeks since any of them had slept in a proper bed.

"I was wondering, Miss Delacroix," said Alexandra delicately, "if you had any baggage that we should collect."

The color in Isobel's cheeks grew more intense. "Thank you, Miss Lytton, but—but we are carrying all of our baggage with us."

"Well, in that case, why don't you leave your belongings in your rooms before we go down to eat?" She opened the doors to both chambers, and the children went cheerfully in to deposit their satchels and packs. Isobel and Ned were to share a room, while Clarissa would look after Jennifer.

She settled the children at a table, and very soon they were served with rook pie, vegetable pudding, sliced ham, and a Cheddar cheese, followed by plum cake. Ned in particular was greatly struck by the plum cake and made his way to the kitchen to pay his compliments to the cook, returning with another slice. Even Jenny ate, and she managed to smile at Alexandra at the close of the meal when the children thanked her.

"I see that you are readers," Alexandra observed approvingly. Clarissa had carried a book with her from her room, and Jenny also had a small, thick book bound in red leather. "I know that Clarissa is reading *Waverley*. What are you reading, Jennifer?"

Alarmed by her interest, Jennifer picked up her book from the table and clutched it to her chest. "Nothing," she said in a low voice, not meeting Alexandra's eyes.

Isobel, feeling an obligation to the woman who had been so generous to them, said in a low voice, "It is a diary. It belonged to our grandmother, and Jenny carries it with her everywhere."

"I see," said Alexandra, smiling at Jenny encouragingly.

"I once kept a diary myself, but I'm afraid that I wasn't very good at it. I could never think of anything interesting to write about. I should imagine that your grandmother wrote very well, though, since you like to carry her diary with you and read it."

Jenny smiled at her and nodded.

"It actually *is* very well written," contributed Clarissa. "Of course, it's not so exciting as *Waverley*, but then you could not expect that."

Isobel, whose mind was on more serious topics, turned to Alexandra and spoke in a low voice. "Do you know when Michael will be able to travel again, Miss Lytton?"

She shook her head. "Mr. Jameson, the surgeon, will be back later today, and I daresay he will be able to tell us something then."

Isobel nodded and stared across the table at nothing in particular.

"What is troubling you, Miss Delacroix?" asked Alexandra gently. "Is there anything that I may do to help you?"

"Oh no, Miss Lytton—you have already been more than kind to us, especially to Michael, and I don't know how we can repay you."

"I don't expect any repayment. I did what I wished to do. But please do confide in me what your plans are now. When you asked about Michael traveling, where were you thinking of going?"

Isobel hesitated, obviously uncertain of how much she should tell. Watching Clarissa reading to Jenny within the comfort of four walls and Ned dining on more plum cake, her resolve crumbled.

"We are trying to find our uncle, Miss Lytton, in the hope that he will offer us a home with him."

"You have an uncle?" asked Alexandra, greatly cheered by the news. "Where does he live?"

"That is our difficulty," said Isobel. "We aren't precisely certain."

Her story emerged slowly. The children had lived in Boston with their widowed mother until her sudden death over a year ago.

"What happened then?" asked Alexandra gently. "Were you sent to an orphanage?"

Isobel shook her head. "Mama had a little money and a house, and our neighbor said that we could live with him and his wife if we signed over the property to him."

The children had wanted to stay together, so they had agreed. It had turned out to be a disastrous decision. They were poorly cared for, and the neighbor had appropriated most of the money for himself.

The others were now listening to the conversation, and Clarissa spoke up at this point. "The only reason we had any money at all is because of Isobel. She took Mama's jewelry and clock and hid them. When we got ready to leave, she and Michael sold them."

"And so you ran away," said Alexandra, thinking about how difficult all this had been for them.

Clarissa shook her head. "We aren't running away from something as much as we are running toward something."

"To your uncle?"

They all nodded.

"And have you ever met him?"

"No," replied Isobel. "Our mother told us about him, so we have heard stories about him all our lives. He and our mother were twins."

"And you're going to their birthplace? Is that where you expect to find your uncle?"

"Oh, no!" they chorused, shaking their heads.

"They were born in France, where our father lived," Isobel explained. "Our mother never set foot in England."

Alexandra thought about this for a moment. "Then your mother had received letters from your uncle that had been sent from England?"

Again they shook their heads. "She didn't speak of any letters, and we didn't find any after Mama died," said Isobel.

"Then how do you hope to find him?" she asked, completely puzzled. "Surely you aren't just going from town to town looking for him? And how can you be certain that he *is* in England?"

There was a brief pause, then Ned nudged Jennifer. "Tell her, Jenny. You're the one who thought of where he would be."

"Ned's right," said Clarissa. "Mama had told us that she was certain that our uncle went to England as soon as she ran away to marry Papa. She was only sixteen then, but she was very unhappy, and so was her brother. But it was Jenny who thought of where in England he would be."

"Well, I must confess that I'm now completely lost," confessed Alexandra. "How did you solve the problem, Jenny?"

Jennifer patted the red leather diary. "I read this," she said in a low voice. "We found it in Mama's desk."

"And what did you discover in your grandmother's diary?" asked Alexandra gently.

"She wrote about how much she loved her home, the place where she grew up," responded Jenny, smiling slightly. "She wrote about it all the time, telling about how it looked and what she did there when she was little."

"Our grandmother ran away to get married, too," explained Clarissa. "It seems to run in the family. But our grandmother missed her home and her parents."

"Did she ever go back to visit?" asked Alexandra.

Jennifer shook her head. "But she told our mama and

her brother about her home, just like she wrote about it in her diary. We think that's where our uncle went."

"Do you know where her home was?"

"Almost," said Isobel. "Our grandmother lived in the country, but she went to local balls at the Assembly Rooms in a town called Shellingham, so her home must have been nearby."

"Do you know anything else?" asked Alexandra, feeling much more hopeful now.

Clarissa nodded. "We know the name of her childhood home. Tell Miss Lytton what it is, Jenny."

Jenny smiled. "Greengage Manor. They named it for the plum trees that grow there."

CHAPTER 7

Richard Browning, Pamela, and Mrs. Wingate were all enjoying an elegant dinner—*inside* the house in the dining room—when a footman appeared and said something to Butterworth in a low voice. Pamela, who had noted this exchange, was astonished to see the butler stare at his master for a moment, then turn and hobble from the room more swiftly than she had thought possible. In a short time he reappeared and hurried to Browning's side. After a few words, Browning rose abruptly, excused himself to his guests, and strode from the room.

"Richard, whatever is happening?" Pamela called. But the door to the dining room had already closed behind him.

She and her mother stared at one another. "What extraordinary behavior! And Richard is *never* rude!" remarked Mrs. Wingate.

The two women made a pretence of eating for the next few minutes, but finally Pamela rose from her chair and marched to the door. "I simply can't sit here and wait, Mother," she announced. "I *must* know what has caused such a fuss in the midst of our dinner. It is really quite inexcusable."

She could hear voices coming from the drawing room and she moved quickly toward them, her silk skirt rustling busily. Butterworth stood just outside the open doors to the room, still looking uncharacteristically agitated, and a footman and maid were hurrying up the stairs on some unknown errand.

Pamela paused in the doorway and looked in disbelief at the scene before her. To her astonishment, her fiancé appeared to be entertaining part of a gypsy camp. A closer inspection revealed that the group appeared to consist entirely of gypsy children. The girls were not wearing the bright jewelry she expected of Romanies, but the children were all dark-haired and dark-eyed, their complexions dusky. They were most certainly as dusty and ragged as people were who lived on the open road, and one of them wore a jacket of Turkey red. The very strangest thing about the collection of children, however, was that one of them was covered by a blanket and lying on the floor, apparently having been carried in on a makeshift stretcher. Next to him, on one of the Aubusson carpets, was a small heap of packs and satchels.

"Richard, what in the name of heaven is the meaning of all this?" she demanded indignantly. Seeing these unkempt children in their dusty clothes seated on the brocade sofa and velvet chairs horrified her. The furniture would be ruined.

"Why are these people in our *drawing* room? Beggars are sent to the kitchen door! Butterworth must have taken leave of his senses to allow them to be brought in here!"

Browning turned to her stiffly. "Pamela, apparently I have the somewhat dubious pleasure of introducing you to my family."

Her expression indicated that Butterworth might not be the only one whose faculties were disordered.

Seeing her stunned reaction, Browning nodded pleasantly. "I received the news in much the same way."

Pamela sat down abruptly on the nearest chair. "What

are you talking about, Richard? You have no family. You told me that your grandmother died several years ago."

"Yes, that is true," he agreed. "And I did intend to tell you about my sister, but I had not gotten to that yet—and there seemed to be no great rush since I had not seen her nor heard from her in some eighteen years."

"Your *sister?*" repeated Pamela blankly. Then, glancing about the room, she saw Alexandra for the first time, and took stock of her. Her complexion was fair and her eyes blue, but her hair was as dark as that of the children.

Browning, following her glance, shook his head. "This is not my sister, Pamela. Reeva, I understand, died last year in America. This is—this is Miss Alexandra Lytton, whom we have to thank for bringing my nieces and nephews to us."

He turned to Alexandra. "Miss Lytton, allow me to present my fiancée, Miss Wingate."

Alexandra, feeling all the tension of a very awkward situation and filled with anger at Richard Browning for his cold reception of the children, merely nodded to Pamela. Pamela, however, was not able to manage even that much. Instead, she turned back toward Browning.

"Richard, this *cannot* be true! Why ever has Miss—Miss Layden brought these children *here?*"

"Apparently because I am their only living relative," he explained briefly, and once again an uncomfortable silence fell on the room.

As the implication of his statement dawned upon Pamela, she stood up abruptly. "Surely you don't mean to take these children in, Richard! Why, there are"—here she stopped and counted. "There are *five* of them!"

"Are you suggesting, Miss Wingate, that it would somehow be more acceptable if there were four of them or seven of them?" inquired Alexandra in a deceptively sweet voice. Thus far, the children's reception had been a nightmare, and this woman promised to be the crowning blow.

"Pray don't be ridiculous! Of course I was not suggesting such a thing, although I simply cannot see how I can be expected to take care of *five*—"

"Nothing has been said about your taking care of anyone, Pamela," said Browning. "Naturally I would not expect you to be burdened with the care of these children."

"Yes, but if you must take them in—but then you *don't* mean to do so, do you, Richard?" she asked, relief flooding her voice. "I knew that you were too sensible a man to consider doing such a ridiculous thing!"

"Ridiculous to take in your own family, Miss Wingate?" inquired Alexandra, watching with dismay the expressions of the children as they heard themselves discussed with such brutal frankness.

"How do we even know they *are* Richard's nieces and nephews?" demanded Pamela.

Alexandra glanced pointedly from the children to Richard Browning. Their coloring was the same, and his nose and brow were markedly like Michael's. Anyone could see that they were related.

"Yes, I can certainly see how you might wonder that," she replied.

Pamela flushed, but then focused on Michael, whose eyes had been closed for most of the exchange. "And why is that boy lying on the floor?"

"That is a very good question," said Alexandra, before anyone else could reply. "I am touched that you are concerned for his welfare, Miss Wingate, and it *does* indeed seem to me that he should be in a bed."

"That is being looked after, Miss Lytton," said Browning, reentering the conversation after a whispered conference with Butterworth. "A bed is ready for him now. My butler will oversee having the footmen carry him up, and I have sent for a surgeon to come and check on his condition as soon as possible."

"A surgeon? Why does the boy need a surgeon?" asked Pamela.

"It appears that my nephew was shot," replied Browning pleasantly. "I believe that he was attempting to rob a carriage at gunpoint."

Pamela sat down and slumped against the back of her chair in a very unladylike posture, for the moment forgetting entirely to arrange herself in the most becoming pose possible. The footmen entered to carry Michael from the room, and the children and Alexandra rose to go with them. Butterworth hovered about the stretcher, urging the footmen to carry the boy carefully.

"Miss Lytton, if you will be so good as to remain with me, I should like to speak with you in private," said Browning, his tone one of command rather than request.

Alexandra colored slightly, but she nodded courteously and seated herself once more. When Isobel glanced over her shoulder nervously as she left the room, Alexandra smiled at her.

"I shall be with you directly," she told the girl, who smiled gratefully.

As the last of the children left the drawing room, Browning turned to her abruptly. "And just why, Miss Lytton, do you take it upon yourself to tell my niece that you will be with her directly?" he demanded. "This is not your home, so how do you presume to make free with what you do here?"

Alexandra looked at him in astonishment, then with mounting indignation. "I presume to do so, sir, because I have an interest in the welfare of those children! The niece to whom I spoke—and her name is Isobel; I daresay you didn't note that—has managed to bring her brothers and sisters hundreds of miles to find you, facing dangers and fears that you and I can only imagine! Now that they have found you, rather than receiving them with kindness, you treat them as though they are millstones about your neck! You are either a man of little imagination or one of great selfishness!"

Browning's jaw had tightened noticeably as she spoke, but before he had the opportunity to retort, Alexandra had risen from her chair and marched toward the door.

"I am going up now to oversee Michael's care and— assuming, of course, that you are going to provide shelter for the others at least for the night—to arrange for their care as well. You may find me upstairs if you wish to speak with me further!" And she turned and walked from the room.

"Well, of all the ill-bred impertinence!" gasped Pamela. "Richard, you must go after that woman and have her ejected from the house at once! That was intolerable behavior!"

Browning, who had been overcome by a wave of anger that he had not felt in years, did not immediately reply. Forcing himself to breathe more slowly and deeply, he walked to the window and looked out toward the orchards.

"Yes, it was," he said, in a voice too low for her to hear. "Quite intolerable."

"Richard, are you attending to what I am saying?" Pamela had risen and walked to stand beside him. "We cannot have that creature in the house! It's bad enough that those children are here, at least for the moment, but *she* most certainly cannot remain!"

When he did not respond, she started toward the door. "I shall see to the matter myself!" she announced. "I am fully capable of having that woman removed from the premises!"

"No, Pamela!" he replied, his voice sharp. "I will take care of the matter myself!"

"I should hope so!" she sniffed. "After all, it is *our* house, and you are master here!"

To her astonishment, he began to laugh and looked out at the orchards once more. Pamela waited a moment, but when he said nothing more, she left the drawing room and climbed the stairs. The bustle of servants going up and down from the third floor immediately indicated where she would find the children and Miss Lytton.

Michael had been removed from the stretcher and placed in a high bed on clean, soft sheets, where he lay with his eyes closed, obviously exhausted by the journey from The Gray Goose. The other children stood together in a miserable knot, as close to the bedside as they could manage. Alexandra was bathing his forehead with a cool cloth and wondering if she and Mr. Jameson had made the correct decision.

The surgeon, who had heard of Greengage Manor and knew its direction, had felt that moving the boy there was the wisest thing they could do. Alexandra had the use of the coach for at least the next day, and so she could transport him as quickly and comfortably as possible. The infection had lessened overnight, and his fever had all but disappeared.

It had been a risk, of course, because their uncle might be away, but Alexandra feared that without the help of the two servants and the carriage, she might not be able to manage moving them, nor could she afford to keep all of them at The Gray Goose indefinitely. With Mr. Jameson's blessing, it had seemed the only course of action possible.

Now, however, looking down at his gaunt face, the pallor showing even through his dusky skin, she was less certain that she had acted in his best interests—or, indeed, in the best interests of any of the children. Their reception at Greengage Manor had been very far from what they had hoped for.

They had decided on their journey there that all of the children should go in with Alexandra. At first, they had thought that having just Isobel go with her would be best, so that their uncle would not have the shock of seeing such a crowd at one time, but the others did not want to be left in the carriage. And most certainly they could not all go in and leave Michael alone. The final vote had been that they would present a united front.

Alexandra had regretted the fact that there had not been time to purchase new clothing for the children. She could not even lend Isobel one of her own gowns, for the girl was far too short for one to fit. All she could do was to have them clean up as much as possible and then put on their old clothing, brushed as clean as they could manage. She could not even have the maids at the inn wash the clothing because much of it had grown so thin that it would have torn during the washing. Finally, since she had no other choice, she had decided that it would be good for their uncle to see just how difficult their journey had been. That, she thought, must melt the hardest of hearts.

When Richard Browning strode into the drawing room, he had stopped two steps inside the door and stared from one face to another. Alexandra caught her breath and looked at him in disbelief, for here was the man who had waltzed with her, the man whose smiling eyes she still occasionally saw in a pleasant daydream. His eyes were not smiling now, however.

Finally she had stood and introduced herself and then had introduced each of the children. Still he had said nothing. She could have forgiven his astonishment, for certainly he had no reason to expect either

her appearance or an onslaught of small relatives that bore a striking resemblance to him. What she could not forgive was his treatment of the children.

Clarissa, seeing his shock, had tried to help him, saying, "We are your sister Reeva's children, you see."

That seemed to bring him from his trance, but instead of responding in any way they might have expected, he answered harshly, "I have no sister! She died long ago."

Ned shook his head manfully, determined to correct the misunderstanding. "No, Uncle Richard. Our mother died just last year."

"So far as I am concerned, my sister died eighteen years ago." He had spoken harshly once more, and the children had looked at one another in confusion, except for Michael, who was drifting in and out of sleep.

"What's wrong with the boy?" he asked abruptly.

"He was shot through the shoulder," Alexandra informed him briskly, trying to establish a more matter-of-fact mood. "He was trying to earn enough money for food for all of them, so he was young and foolish enough to join a pair of highwaymen who tried to rob me. Michael managed to keep the others from hurting my coachman badly—or perhaps even killing him—but he was injured himself in the process."

Browning looked anything but gratified by this news. "How splendid," he replied dryly. "I have a nephew who is already showing signs of going to the devil. Given a few more years, I daresay he will do it properly."

"What a foolish and unnecessary thing to say," replied Alexandra, her voice becoming icy. She had felt shock ripple through the children at their uncle's words, and was grateful that Michael appeared to be soundly asleep.

Browning had looked up at her sharply, intending to put her in her place with a glance, but the dark blaze of his eyes met cold blue flint, and for a moment he had appeared almost amused.

Isobel, swallowing hard, had entered the fray. "Miss Lytton has been kind enough to take care of Michael and the rest of us, and to help us reach Greengage Manor and you, Uncle."

He had looked at Alexandra again. "I can see that I am once again deeply indebted to you, Miss Lytton," he had responded dryly. Fortunately, Miss Wingate did not appear to have heard the "once again" portion of his comment.

He had been anything but kind to the children, but at least, she thought, he was providing them with food and shelter for the moment—no matter how ungraciously he was doing so. His fiancée, however, made him appear an angel of mercy. What a horror the woman was!

At that moment, she glanced up and saw Miss Wingate standing in the doorway. Alexandra had never before seen anyone quiver with indignation, but it appeared to her that Miss Wingate was doing precisely that.

"Butterworth!" Pamela said, her voice sharp and thin. The butler, as she knew, was in the chamber next door, having it readied for one of the strangers who had invaded Greengage Manor.

A minute or two later, he appeared beside her, somewhat breathless from all the bustle. "Yes, Miss Wingate?"

"I believe that Miss Layden is ready to leave now," she said, staring coldly at Alexandra. "Have one of the footmen see her to the door."

"Oh, no!" exclaimed Isobel, turning to Alexandra and putting her hand out to her. "Miss Lytton, please don't leave us yet!"

The younger ones, recognizing the imminent loss of the only stability they had known in months, and their only advocate in the present unhappy situation, gathered around her.

Butterworth turned to Miss Wingate. "I believe, Miss Wingate, that I must speak with Mr. Browning first."

Her back ramrod stiff, Pamela turned and walked away without a word, leaving the children limp with relief.

"We don't want you to leave us, Miss Lytton," said Clarissa fervently. "We don't know anyone here, and no one seems to like us at all. We want you to stay with us."

Alexandra smiled reassuringly at the children, but she was decidedly uneasy. She could not very well stay if she was not invited to do so, and she had certainly seen no sign of such an offer from Mr. Browning—and certainly quite the opposite from his fiancée.

"We will work things out," she told them. "Try not to worry about anything except getting some rest and helping Michael recover."

They had spent the next few minutes getting Michael settled and then settling the others in their rooms. Once they all had found their places, they trooped with her back into Michael's room to be certain that he was sleeping soundly.

Butterworth appeared in the doorway and executed a brief and creaky bow in Alexandra's direction. "If you will allow me, miss, I will show you to your room," he said. "Mr. Browning informed me that you would be staying the night."

Alexandra, taken completely by surprise, smiled at the ancient butler and thanked him. Then she turned to the children, who had heaved a collective sigh of relief.

"I shall be back directly," she told them.

CHAPTER 8

Richard Browning prided himself upon his self-control and his well-ordered life. It had been many years since he had lost control of a situation.

After being left alone in the drawing room, he had needed some time to regain his composure, for he had been completely overset by the cauldron of emotions that had boiled over at the appearance of the children and Miss Lytton.

He had not known that Reeva had borne children. Indeed, so far as he had known, her death could have occurred just after she had run away to be married all those years ago. So far as he had been concerned, she *had* died then.

When he had awakened on their sixteenth birthday and found the note telling him that she had run away with André Delacroix, he had been angry and heartbroken. He had warned her that Delacroix was a ne'er-do-well, and she knew that he had cheated their father out of the last money that they had. He had tried to trace them, but three ships had sailed from Bridgetown that morning—one for Boston, one for Portugal, and one for Bombay. So he had been left penniless and alone with an abusive father who was dying of tuberculosis.

He had remained on Barbados for the two remaining months of his father's life and had seen him buried next to their mother, grateful that she had died before all of this had happened. She had endured enough unhappiness in her short life. The only joy she seemed to have known, apart from her children, was her childhood. He had been delighted by the stories of her girlhood, but Reeva had dismissed them as deadly dull. After her death, he had wanted to find their grandparents, while Reeva said that they would be walking into a trap that would keep them from having any excitement in life.

When Reeva had run away with Delacroix, she had even their taken mother's diary. She had left him nothing.

To be suddenly confronted with her children—two of whom looked remarkably like her—and to hear that she had indeed died had been too much for him. And to have them brought to him by the young woman that he had found so attractive and who had disappeared so mysteriously—and who today had attacked him with some justification—had been the final blow.

Gazing at the orchards brought him no solace now. He straightened his shoulders, knowing that he was going to have to face this problem and solve it. He could not do that by directing his anger at the children and Miss Lytton. His face grew hot as he thought of his earlier behavior toward them.

And Pamela! It suddenly dawned on him that she had been gone for some time, and he had little doubt about what she had been doing. He started for the door, but before he reached it, she rushed into the room, her cheeks and eyes bright with anger.

"Richard, you must direct that woman to leave immediately and you *certainly* must instruct your butler that he is to take orders from me!"

Browning chose to ignore her second demand and to address himself to the first one.

"Pamela, I fear that all of this has quite overset both of

us. We must remember our responsibilities. The children are my family and Miss Lytton my guest. I must not behave otherwise—nor may you."

Ignoring her gasp of indignation, he rang for Butterworth.

CHAPTER 9

Alexandra was pleased to see that Greengage Manor was a well-run household, its staff prepared to accommodate unexpected—and even definitely unwanted—guests. Butterworth showed her to a pleasant room overlooking the garden, where a small maid had just brought in hot water so that she could tidy herself after her journey. Supper trays, she was told, would be brought to her and to the children in their rooms. Butterworth departed after assuring her that her trunk and boxes would be brought up for her, but he reappeared almost immediately.

"Mr. Browning wishes to extend his invitation to join him and his other guests at dinner, Miss Lytton, if you are not too tired from your journey," he informed her, bowing.

Shock kept her from making an immediate reply. She could not imagine why she was being invited to dinner when he had so obviously been extremely angry with her. Then she remembered the carriage and smiled. Of course, he had absolutely no idea who she was—beyond her name—and he doubtless had been informed about the carriage and servants and assumed they belonged to her. Having danced with her at the ball long ago, he would believe her to be a lady of some social standing.

Her first inclination was to refuse and to indulge herself in a well-deserved rest. Then she thought of the children and decided that she should take advantage of this opportunity to speak with him about them. As soon as he discovered that she was a mere governess, she would become persona non grata, so she should do what she could for the children now.

"I'm afraid that I am not dressed for dinner," she replied, ruefully indicating the poplin carriage gown she had worn for travel.

"Mr. Browning said that you were welcome to come as you are, miss, or that they will be happy to wait for you should you wish to change."

Alexandra was astonished by this display of graciousness, even taking the Treemore equipage into consideration. For a moment she thought of the young man she had danced with, but she dismissed that. That man belonged entirely to daydreams.

"Please tell Mr. Browning that I will join them immediately," she said.

A footman had come up behind Butterworth, carrying her trunk, and another followed with her bandboxes. While the little maid unpacked her trunk—a gesture Alexandra thought quite unnecessary, considering the brevity of her stay at Greengage—she washed her face and hands and then brushed her hair, catching it up with golden combs and quickly fastening golden ear loops. She was grateful that her dark dress, if not smart, was at least well-cut and of good quality material, and she picked up the India shawl that Alicia had given her as a parting gift. Then she hurried down the passage to tell the children that she would check on them after dinner.

Butterworth had informed her that she would find the others already in the dining room, and he waited in the flagstoned hall at the foot of the stairway to direct her there. Alexandra knew that the butler had summoned his master from the dinner table when she and

the children arrived, so she shuddered to think of the
state of the dinner and the state of Mr. Browning's mood
by now.

However, Mr. Browning stood and bowed as she entered, and a footman hurried to hold her chair for her.

"Mrs. Wingate, I would like to present Miss Lytton," he
said to Pamela's mother, and the two ladies nodded
stiffly to one another. "And of course, Miss Wingate, you
and Miss Lytton have already met."

That, thought Alexandra, was quite an understatement, but she forced herself to smile and nod to
Pamela Wingate, who acted as though she could not
see Alexandra at the table.

"You must forgive us, Miss Lytton," said Browning in a
remarkably pleasant tone, having reverted to his normal
gentlemanly manner. "We were just finishing our soup
when you and the children arrived, but yours is being
brought now, and our next course will be brought when
you are ready."

Alexandra saw that it would be useless to protest that
she did not need the soup and would happily join them
in the second course so that they need not wait. A footman was bearing down upon her, and so she addressed
herself to the turtle soup, doing her best to ignore the
icy atmosphere.

"We have had a lovely time here, Richard," observed
Mrs. Wingate. "I look forward to returning for the house
party. Pamela was just saying that it was a thousand pities
that we could not spend more time here now." This,
naturally, was stretching the truth quite thin, but Mrs.
Wingate could see no immediate problem with that, and
she ignored her daughter's quick glance.

"It appears that your wish to spend a little more time
at Greengage has been granted," replied Browning,
gazing impassively at Alexandra. "I will need to remain

here for a few days in order to make arrangements for the children."

Both Alexandra and Pamela looked up sharply at this.

"A few days! But, Richard, we were to return to town tomorrow!" Pamela protested. "We do have so much to do to prepare for the ball—and of course we have other engagements as well!"

"Yes, I realize that, my dear, but I can hardly leave for London tomorrow morning after what has happened. I'm certain you see that some provision must be made for the children."

The mulish set of Miss Wingate's pretty mouth indicated that she saw nothing of the sort.

"Pamela tells me that there are five children," said Mrs. Wingate, anxious to smooth the ruffled waters. "And they are, apparently—" Here she paused, trying to think of a tactful way to phrase it. "They apparently are in need of new sets of clothing."

"Indeed they are," agreed Alexandra. "They have quite worn out everything they were able to bring with them on their journey."

"How very extraordinary that they should undertake such a thing by themselves," said Mrs. Wingate. "I cannot understand why they were not accompanied by a servant. It is most unsuitable for such young children to be traveling alone."

"I know very little about the circumstances that led to their journey," said Browning, looking at Alexandra. "Perhaps you could enlighten me, Miss Lytton."

"Yes, it does seem very odd, their arriving here with you, Miss Lytton," agreed Mrs. Wingate.

Alexandra did her best to sketch the children's situation after their mother's death, hoping that her listeners would be appropriately moved. Mr. Browning listened carefully, his dark eyes intent upon her, while Miss Wingate appeared to be staring at a portrait of some long-dead relation of Mr. Browning. Her mother, however, was unmistakably listening.

"They sold their mother's jewelry?" she exclaimed in horror, after Alexandra had explained how they had financed their trip across the Atlantic. "That should have been kept for her daughters! It never should have been allowed to leave the family!"

"I don't believe that they felt they had a choice, ma'am," explained Alexandra gently. "If they had not done so, they would have remained at their neighbor's mercy, without being sent to school or having any expectation of a future. They were little better than bond servants to him."

Mrs. Wingate could only stare at her with horror-stricken eyes. So struck was she by their plight that she allowed the footman to pour her another glass of claret.

"I did not know that people of our class ever lived in such a manner," she said.

"But, as we see, it *does* happen," replied Browning shortly.

Pamela finally spoke, indicating that she had, after all, been listening. "Even if they are your sister's children, Richard, you cannot be expected to accept children from such a background into your home. That is asking far too much of you—and of me."

"And what provision would you make for them, Pamela?" he asked quietly.

She colored slightly. "Well, after the menial labor that they have been doing, they could be sent into service somewhere—perhaps in Scotland, where you could find them good jobs and they would be far away."

"Pamela, have you lost your senses?" demanded her mother.

Alexandra looked at Mrs. Wingate in surprise. She

herself had been shocked by the suggestion, but she had not expected the same reaction from Mrs. Wingate.

That lady was looking at her daughter in disbelief. "Do you know, Pamela, just what it would mean to you and Richard—and to me—if it were known that you had family in *service?*" Her voice rose hysterically at the final word.

"You need not trouble yourself, ma'am," Browning said quietly. "I would not allow that to happen."

"You see, Mother," said Pamela triumphantly. "Richard can handle it in such a manner that no one need ever know."

"That is not what I meant, Pamela. I meant that I will not allow my sister's children to be treated in such a manner."

Alexandra leaned back and breathed a sigh of relief. She had feared that he would do precisely what Miss Wingate was suggesting.

"Then what *do* you plan to do with them, Richard?" Pamela demanded.

He shook his head. "I haven't yet decided."

The surgeon arrived as the pheasant pie was being served, and Browning excused himself once more to his guests. Alexandra also rose to leave, and Pamela spoke abruptly, addressing her for the first time since she had come to the table.

"I'm certain that Mr. Browning and the surgeon have no need of your presence, Miss Layden," she said.

Alexandra flushed slightly. "Perhaps not. But I am quite certain that Michael and the children do." With that, she left the room, following quietly in Browning's wake.

The surgeon inspected Michael's wound, put on a fresh dressing, and advised him to rest. Since Michael was already drifting off to sleep once more, the advice appeared unnecessary, but Alexandra was glad to see that it was a natural sleep this time, rather than a drug-induced one.

After the surgeon had taken his leave, Alexandra said, "If you will excuse me, sir, I don't believe that I will go down to dinner again. I am quite tired, and after I check on the children, I am going to my room."

He nodded. "Certainly. The maid will be in to see if you need anything more."

She smiled her thank you and turned toward Jennifer and Clarissa's chamber door.

"Miss Lytton, before I go, I need to offer you an apology for my boorish behavior when you arrived."

His manner was stiff and it was clear that the words cost him considerable effort, but his voice was sincere. "I was—taken by surprise, but that is no excuse. I know that you have gone to considerable trouble to help the children, and I want you to know that—despite what I said earlier, I am deeply appreciative."

"It is good of you to apologize to me, Mr. Browning." She looked him squarely in the eye as she spoke. "However, I think that it is far more important that you apologize to the children. They are the ones who can be deeply hurt by your words—and your actions."

Browning met her gaze and held it. "I know that you are correct, Miss Lytton, but—it will be difficult. And it may take me a little time."

"Do you plan to keep them here with you, sir?"

He did not look down, but he did not answer immediately. Finally he nodded. "Yes, I believe I will—at least for a time."

Alexandra smiled at him. "Then you will have time to make your peace with them, Mr. Browning."

Turning, she knocked softly on the girls' door and let herself quietly into their room.

CHAPTER 10

The day had ended far better than she had dreamed it could. The children were safely settled at Greengage Manor—for the moment, at least—and Michael was under the care of a competent surgeon who had made a very optimistic report. His brother and three sisters had eaten, bathed, and settled securely—once again, at least for the moment—in their bedchambers. And, best of all, it appeared that Mr. Browning planned to meet his responsibility to his family.

She herself was comfortably ensconced in her chamber, and she had spoken with Davis, who was to take the carriage back to London tomorrow. She could take the stagecoach home to Torquay.

In the meantime, she knew that the children slept better knowing that they had a friend in the house. Before she left, she would do her best to be certain that Richard Browning had a proper attitude toward the new additions to his household. Despite his obvious distress about the appearance of the children and some ancient quarrel with his sister, she felt that he was not a heartless man.

Her thoughts about his fiancée were something else again. She could see quite clearly that Miss Wingate had little interest in anyone save herself. That did not, she knew, augur well for the children. It was entirely possi-

ble, however, that since Mr. Browning had decided that
keeping the children was indeed his duty, he would be
able to convince his fiancée to accept them. Given what
she had seen of Miss Wingate, however, she very much
doubted that anyone could persuade her to be kind to
them. Unfortunately, Alexandra could think of nothing
she could do to remedy that problem.

Alexandra's sleep that night, like that of Richard
Browning, was fitful. If she dreamed of waltzing and dark,
laughing eyes, it was only to be expected. She knew, however, the clear demarcation between dreams and reality.
Her life had taught her that.

When the first rays of sunlight appeared, she dressed,
slipped into her pelisse, and walked outside. In spite of
her troubled state of mind when they had arrived yesterday, she had seen immediately how lovely Greengage
Manor was. She could understand why the children's
grandmother had remembered it and written about it
so fondly. How sad it was to think that she had never
returned to it.

She walked toward the orchards, enjoying the fresh-
ness of the morning and the tranquility of the scene
before her. She hoped that Richard Browning would indeed keep them here—and that Miss Wingate would
allow it once they were married. She was not certain
what she thought of him. Certainly he seemed to have
shown two very different sides of himself yesterday. Miss
Wingate, on the other hand, unfortunately appeared to
have only one. She smiled to herself, thinking of Ned,
who had said Miss Wingate was like the cruel mother in
Hansel and Gretel, who encourages their father to send
them out into the woods so that they can't find their way
back home. Before she left for Torquay, she would have
to tell him that it would be better if he did not say that
within anyone else's hearing.

When she reached the edge of the greengage orchard, she sat down on a low stone wall so that she could enjoy its beauty, the blossoms glowing gently in the rising sun. She wondered, as she always did at places such as this, what it felt like to grow up in the midst of such beauty, and to know that your family had lived here for generations and would continue to do so for generations to come. She had been left an orphan when she was only three, and an elderly aunt, her only family, had taken her in. Her aunt had taught French and Italian in a seminary for young ladies, and Alexandra had shared her set of rooms for seventeen years, until her aunt's death. She had received a solid education from her aunt, and had been hired by the seminary to finish her aunt's classes the term that she died. Alexandra had done so, and it was there that Mrs. Treemore had met her and hired her as Alicia's governess. Her whole life, it seemed, had been spent living in other people's homes.

"You appear lost in thought, Miss Lytton," said Browning, who swung himself over the wall and sat down beside her.

"Yes, I was. It is beautiful out here. I can't imagine what it must feel like to be able to look at all of this anytime you wish."

Browning, staring out into the plum blossoms as she was, nodded. "I find myself thinking the same thing and then reminding myself that I can. It is a constant source of joy."

Alexandra remembered what the children had told her about their uncle—that he had been born in France and that, like his sister Reeva, had never been to Greengage Manor during his childhood. The earliest he could possibly have come was when he was already sixteen, so doubtless what he said was true. He didn't take his blessings for granted.

"I can see that it would be," she agreed. "I shall carry this scene in my mind for rainy days."

Browning laughed. "Yes, it makes an effective talisman against gray days and unhappiness."

"The children will love it here," she commented, deciding to venture out onto thin ice. After all, she had only a little time before she left, and she must do what she could for them.

Browning was silent for a moment. "I hope that they will, and we will at least try it for a while—although it may seem a little too tame for someone who has already tried his hand at highway robbery."

She laughed. "When you get to know Michael, I daresay that you will be devoted to him. His brother and sisters are."

He nodded. "He is doubtless like his mother—completely charming and utterly thoughtless."

Before she could respond, he turned to her and asked, "Why did you not wait for me to waltz with you again, Miss Lytton? You disappeared as completely as if you had been a part of a magician's performance. I almost convinced myself that I imagined our dancing together."

Alexandra met his gaze for a moment, then dropped her eyes. "I was called away," she replied.

He waited for her to continue, but when she did not, he rose abruptly and said, "Breakfast will be served by now, Miss Lytton. I should imagine you wish to come in from the damp and have something to eat."

She stood up and looked down ruefully at the hem of her muslin gown, soaked by morning dew. "You are quite right, Mr. Browning. I believe a warm fire and a cup of chocolate will be welcome."

They walked back to the house in an uneasy silence; nonetheless, Alexandra felt more and more hopeful about the children's future. Just why he had shown such anger when they first arrived was not entirely clear, but he appeared to have himself well in hand now, and she found him well-bred and intelligent. Considering what she had seen of the Delacroix children, that was scarcely surprising.

When she had changed her frock and put on dry slippers, Alexandra went to check on the children once more. They were all still soundly asleep, and she went down to breakfast in a more cheerful frame of mind than she had known since the night of the attempted holdup.

"I do think, Richard, that we should be leaving this morning for London," Pamela Wingate was saying fretfully as Alexandra entered the breakfast room.

"You know that I must be here for the next day or so, Pamela," he reminded her gently. Then he turned toward Alexandra. "Good morning again, Miss Lytton."

"Again?" said Pamela, not addressing Alexandra at all.

"I encountered Miss Lytton on an early morning walk," he said pleasantly. "It appears that we both enjoy the orchard at dawn."

"How delightful," replied Pamela, in a voice that indicated it was anything but delightful.

"Yes, it certainly was," said Alexandra brightly, just as though Miss Wingate had made her comment sincerely. She served herself from the sideboard, and a footman brought her a cup of chocolate. "I am delighted to see the fire," she said to Browning. "I had forgotten how chilly spring mornings can be when the dew is heavy."

Pamela sniffed. "I am surprised to see that you are not wearing the gold loops in your ears this morning, Miss Lytton," she said, finally saying Alexandra's name correctly.

Alexandra looked up at her in surprise. "My gold

loops? Why are you surprised that I'm not wearing them, Miss Wingate?"

Pamela smiled sweetly. "Why, because they make you look almost like a gypsy, despite your complexion. I had thought that perhaps you were attempting to look more like the children by wearing them."

"Indeed?" replied Alexandra politely. "I should be very happy to resemble the Delacroix children. They are quite charming."

Butterworth entered and bowed to Alexandra. "Miss Lytton, your coachman wishes to know if you have any final instructions for him before his departure."

From the corner of her eye she could see the other two look up in surprise at the butler's words.

"No, thank you, Butterworth. If you will, please, simply give him my thanks and my wish for a safe journey home."

As Butterworth left, Pamela eyed her speculatively. "How very odd, Miss Lytton. Why is your carriage leaving without you, and why would you thank your coachman?"

"It is not my carriage, Miss Wingate," responded Alexandra, sipping her chocolate. "Nor are the coachman and footman my servants."

"Stranger still," observed Pamela. "Why ever were you riding about the countryside in someone else's carriage?"

She flushed slightly at the impertinence of the questions, but she replied calmly. "I had been to a wedding in London, and the carriage was returning me to my home in Torquay, when I encountered the children."

"When Michael attempted to rob you," Browning corrected. "And so you live in Torquay, Miss Lytton?"

"For the moment," she replied. "Or, more correctly, for the next two months." Then, deciding that she might as well bite the bullet now as later, she continued. "I am a governess, you see, and I am presently on holiday. I will go to a new post after that."

"A governess?" said Pamela, clearly amused. "A governess jaunting about the countryside in a private carriage?"

"I cannot see anything so strange about that, Pamela," said Browning reprovingly.

"Well, of course she is quite right, Mr. Browning." Alexandra looked at him and spoke frankly. "Governesses certainly cannot afford to keep their own carriages. One of my former employers provided it for my use."

"Pray tell us why you did not keep the carriage here to carry you to Torquay." Pamela was regarding her with raised brows. "Are you planning to stay on here with us?"

"I had kept the carriage quite long enough. I plan to take the stagecoach to Torquay." Alexandra did not allow herself to be ruffled by the tone of either Miss Wingate's question or her voice.

"Of course you will not travel by coach," said Browning. "You will travel post. You would have already been comfortably home if you had not broken your journey to look after my nieces and nephews."

"That is very kind of you, Mr. Browning, but most unnecessary." Alexandra smiled at him gratefully, and did not deny herself the pleasure of glancing at Miss Wingate's pretty pout at this unexpected turn of the conversation. Her pout grew more pronounced almost immediately, however.

Mr. Browning suddenly leaned toward Alexandra, his eyes alight. "Miss Lytton, discovering that you are a governess is the greatest stroke of good fortune! Could I possibly convince you to give up a few more days of your holiday and remain with us here? I am not experienced with children, and your help would be invaluable!"

"Richard!" gasped Pamela. "How could you make such an offer without consulting me first?"

Alexandra had not considered such a possibility, so she was not prepared for his request and did not respond at all.

Browning turned back to Pamela to console her. "Do be sensible, Pamela." His voice was tender, rather than exasperated. "Don't you see that this would give us a great deal more freedom at a time when we have so much to do?"

A little more murmuring finally won a reluctant smile from his bride-to-be, and he turned back to Alexandra.

"Will you please consider it, Miss Lytton? I know that it is yet another imposition, but we would be most grateful and I would pay you well for your time."

For a moment Alexandra thought longingly of walks by the sea and of time for herself. Then she saw Jennifer and Ned peeking around the door to the breakfast room, trying to catch her eye.

"Very well, Mr. Browning," she said, laughing. "I shall stay for a few days to help you set things to rights."

CHAPTER 11

"Well, I suppose that it is better than having to take care of the raggle-taggle gypsies ourselves," conceded Pamela, watching Alexandra with Ned and Jennifer. "Surely she can at least get them some decent clothes and make them look reasonably respectable. I do *not* think, however, that they should be here at all. No one would expect it of you, Richard, save for someone as ridiculous as Miss Lytton."

Browning cleared his throat. "I told you, Pamela, that I had planned to tell you about my sister."

"Yes, I know—but now there's no need, is there? I know about her. And I see that she has left the responsibility of her children to you."

"That would have been her way," admitted Browning, unable to keep an edge of bitterness from his voice, "leaving her responsibilities to others."

"Well, you have absolutely no obligation to assume them, Richard. You must think of *us.*"

Browning did not immediately say whether or not he agreed with her estimate of the situation, although he would very much have liked to be free of the Delacroix children and to have his own life back. He sat back and took a sip of coffee, listening to the laughter of the children as it faded into the distance. Miss Lytton had taken them elsewhere, and already Pamela was feeling more kindly toward her.

"Actually, Pamela," he said at last, when the breakfast room was completely silent, "that is what I needed to tell you about my sister. You see, even if I had no moral obligation to take care of her children, I would have a legal one."

"Why?" demanded Pamela, pausing in her pastime of crumbling toast and sipping tea. "Why do you have a legal responsibility, Richard?"

"My sister Reeva was still alive when my grandmother died, you see."

Pamela waited expectantly for him to continue. When he did not, she said impatiently, "Yes, Richard. I gathered that your sister was still alive then. What does that have to do with your having a legal responsibility?"

He rose and walked over to the window, looking out across the lawn. He couldn't see the orchards from here, and he felt somehow bereft.

Finally he brought himself to say it, still with his back turned. "My grandmother left Greengage to me—and to Reeva."

A brief silence ensued while Pamela thought this over. "Do you mean that you own only *half* of Greengage Manor?"

He nodded, still facing the window. "I planned to tell you, of course, but I didn't think that it really mattered one way or another because I knew that Reeva would never consider coming here. I was absolutely certain that Greengage would always be mine, even though she owned half of it. My grandmother's solicitor couldn't even locate her at the time of our grandmother's death to tell her about her inheritance."

"I don't see that there's any problem now, Richard. After all, Reeva is dead."

"Yes, but her children aren't," he pointed out. "That means that half of Greengage Manor belongs to them."

"Nonsense! They are too young!"

"Youth has nothing to do with the matter, however. I will naturally be completely in charge because they are still minors, but you can see, Pamela, that I most certainly have the responsibility for their care. Half of this estate is their inheritance."

"Even *if* that is true, they need not be cared for *here*," she responded reasonably. "Heaven knows that they need to be educated and to learn manners. They should all be sent away to school—although it sickens me to think how much that will cost for five of them."

She thought it over for a minute or two. "Still, that would be the best thing for us. Seeing them almost destroy that lovely drawing room yesterday was more than I could bear."

Browning smiled faintly, relieved to have unburdened himself of his secret. "I don't believe they destroyed it."

"Then you must not have been looking closely at their clothing, Richard—if you can possibly call the rags they were wearing clothing. I was shocked that you allowed them to be seated in your drawing room."

"Well, my dear, at least you now know about my sister—and about the rest of the family that I didn't know that I had," he said, attempting to change the topic as lightly as possible. "And now I daresay that you and your mother should be working on a list of things that need to be done for the ball. I think that the two of you should go back to London tomorrow, and I will join you in a day or two."

Pamela's face had grown animated at the mention of London. "That would be splendid, Richard! But you must come back with us!"

He shook his head. "I have a few things that must be

done before I leave here. However, I can't see why you and your mother should have to wait for me." He did not add that he would like a little more time to enjoy Greengage— or that he found the necessity of talking more with Miss Lytton inviting.

Pamela would have greatly preferred having her fiancé escort her, but she could not refuse the opportunity of returning to London. She went to share the glad tidings with her mother, and the two ladies settled down to draw up a list of the warehouses and shops they needed to visit immediately upon their return.

Michael was able to sit up for breakfast that morning, propped in a nest of pillows, and was feeling much more himself. Isobel had explained to him what had happened from the time of his accident, and when Alexandra came in, he smiled at her, his eyes merry in his thin, dark face.

"I told you, Belle, that I had found our guardian angel at The Bull and Basket. I know now that she was waiting for me at the tollhouse that night." With a graceful wave of his right hand and a slight inclination of his head, he bowed to her. "I am very grateful to you, ma'am, for taking care of me and for taking care of my family."

Alexandra had thought that, once he was fully awake again, she would give him a brief lecture on the dangers of acting impulsively, but looking at his cheerful expression, she decided that just now it would be water off a duck's back. She would wait for a more auspicious moment to make her point.

Jennifer was sitting next to him on the bed, attempting to feed him breakfast as though he were a complete invalid, Isobel had pulled a chair close to him, and Clarissa had her book out, prepared to read to him when there was a moment of silence. Only one was missing.

"Where is Ned?" asked Alexandra, expecting to hear that he had gone to his chamber to get something for Michael. She turned to Jennifer. "He was with us as we started up the stairs. I went to my chamber for a moment and you came here, Jennifer. Where did your brother go?"

Jennifer looked uncomfortable. "I think to see the puppies."

"Puppies?" Alexandra looked at her, waiting.

After a moment Jennifer nodded slowly. "The maid told us there were puppies in the stables. I think he might have gone there."

"I believe I'd better go and try to find Ned," she said. Undoubtedly there would be no problem with a ten-year-old wandering off on a private estate, and he would be quite safe wherever he went here. Still, her step quickened as she anticipated possible disasters.

Alexandra had not yet been to the stables, but she planned to go there first in her search. Before she reached the foot of the stairway, however, she could tell that she would not have to make her way to the stables. Ned—a very messy Ned, she saw with dismay—was just emerging from the drawing room with an anguished footman in his wake. When Ned saw Alexandra, his dismal expression lightened.

"Miss Lytton, will you help me find him?" he asked, looking a little more hopeful.

Ned was in his worn clothes, since for the moment they were still all he had, but now they were covered with fresh dark mud, as were his hands and face.

"Ned, what happened to you? Who are you trying to find?"

"Rupert!" he answered.

"The dog!" answered the footman at the same time.

Alexandra's heart sank. "Why were you looking for a dog in the drawing room, Ned?"

He looked up at her unhappily. "Rupert ran that way after he slipped out of my hands. The mud made him slick, but then he rolled on the carpet and got most of it off."

She tried not to think of the lovely Aubusson carpets she had noticed yesterday and how they must look now. The footman had summoned Butterworth, who was hurrying in to inspect the extent of the damage.

"Is Rupert one of the puppies from the stables, Ned?"

He nodded. "I took Rupert down to the duck pond to get a drink, but he liked it so much that he jumped in and then he rolled in the mud at the edge. I caught him, though, and I was bringing him in so that Michael could see him, but he got away again."

Alexandra decided that this was not the moment to discuss the propriety of bringing a muddy dog into the house—especially into an establishment such as this one. First she would get Ned safely out of sight and cleaned up. The butler and his staff, she was certain, would do their best with the drawing room, and she was afraid to look at it for herself. And surely the footman would soon find Rupert and remove him to the stables before he could do anything else.

Alexandra had just gotten Ned started up the stairs when they both froze in place. A piercing shriek split the air, and Pamela Wingate, followed closely by a small terrier pup, ran into the hall. Miss Wingate was a vision in a green lawn gown—a gown whose skirt was now patterned by small muddy paw prints. At present the pup was devoting himself to making the pattern more intricate by leaping again at Miss Wingate.

"Someone get this beast!" she cried, trying to push the pup away with her foot.

"Rupert!" Before she could stop him, Ned rushed down to collect the pup, scooping him up just before the footman could snatch him.

"Is this *your* dog?" shrieked Miss Wingate. "Just look what it has done to my gown!"

Browning, having heard the hue and cry in the depths of his library, joined them in the hall. He frowned as he saw the distraught Pamela and then surveyed the damage that had been done to her gown. His dark gaze settled on Ned.

"I'll speak with you in a moment, sir!" he said shortly. Then he turned to Pamela. "Come into the drawing room, my dear. You need to rest for a moment."

Alexandra and Ned glanced at one another in horror. They watched as the pair walked through the drawing room doors and then stopped abruptly. A short but ominous silence ensued; then they heard Miss Wingate's voice.

"I *told* you they would destroy this room, Richard. This is absolute proof that you cannot allow them to stay here."

Browning came striding back into the hall and glowered down at Ned, who was still holding the wriggling puppy.

"Are you responsible for the mess in there?" he demanded.

Ned, dwarfed by his uncle, nodded. "Rupert and I did it," he replied, "but we didn't mean to—and we're sorry."

Browning appeared unimpressed by this admission and apology.

"Rupert?" Browning's voice was all the more frightening because his intense anger seemed so tightly controlled, as though he might explode if someone touched him. "And is *this* Rupert?"

Ned nodded and met his uncle's gaze squarely. "He's my dog."

"Do you mean to say that you brought a *dog* here with you, too?" His dark winged brows rose in disbelief.

This time Ned shook his head, but very slowly.

"I didn't bring Rupert with me. I just got him," he replied in a low voice, holding the pup under his chin. "I got him this morning in the stable."

"You got that animal *here?*" Browning asked incredulously. "Well, if you got him in the stable, I can assure you he's going directly back there."

He reached down to take the pup from Ned, but the boy clutched it closer and backed away.

Before Browning could take another step closer, Alexandra had inserted herself smoothly between them.

"I believe, Mr. Browning, that since you have asked me to look after the children, I should begin now."

He did not have the opportunity to answer because she turned swiftly to Ned.

"You go directly upstairs and give Rupert to Isobel to take care of until I arrive, then go to your chamber and wait for the hot water that I will have sent up for your bath." She pointed to the stairs. "Go quickly."

Ned went, the pup held close to his chest.

Alexandra turned to meet Browning's furious gaze. "How dare you interfere, Miss Lytton?" he asked in a low voice. She could almost hear him grinding his teeth in fury.

Unperturbed, she smiled at him, meeting his gaze as directly as Ned had. "I believe that you asked me to stay and take care of your nieces and nephews, sir. I was merely doing so."

"I did not ask you to interfere in my discipline of them, ma'am." His expression was grim.

"It seemed to me that a moment ago you were a threat to one of my charges, Mr. Browning—one of the charges that you made me responsible for, I might add—so I had no choice but to care for the child first." Alexandra's manner was crisp and efficient.

"Richard!" Are you going to let her ride roughshod over you as she is doing?" Pamela had just walked into the hall after telling the unfortunate Butterworth, who was carefully directing two maids and a footman in cleaning the mud from furniture and carpet, that he must do his work carefully. "She cares nothing for your lovely home. She would gladly see it destroyed by the horde of raggle-taggle gypsies that has overtaken Greengage."

Alexandra acted as though Miss Wingate had not spoken. She kept her gaze directly upon Browning. "If you will excuse me, sir, I need to go and take care of the children."

Without waiting for his permission, she turned and walked up the stairs.

"Well!" She could feel Miss Wingate's indignant gaze boring into her back, but Browning said nothing, and Alexandra kept walking.

It was, she thought, going to be a trying few days. The only reasons she did not march out the door and walk to the nearest coaching inn were the five waiting for her upstairs. Six now, counting Rupert.

When she arrived upstairs, she rang for a maid to bring hot water for Ned and for Rupert. Since Rupert was quite small and had rubbed off almost of his mud already, making him presentable was not as difficult as it might have been. She allowed Ned to help her with the pup, then left him to scrub himself clean. The little maid had volunteered the information that one of the stable boys was about Ned's size, and Alexandra had dispatched her to see if he had a spare shirt and pair of breeches. Ned's muddy boots had been taken downstairs to be dealt with.

Alexandra looked at the state of the muddy clothes that Ned had removed and shook her head. Their first business must be getting new clothes and shoes for the children.

When she went back into Michael's room, she found Rupert being cosseted and made much of by Jennifer and Clarissa. Now that he was clean, it could be seen that he had a cream-colored coat, marked with splashes of brown, and an alert, inquisitive expression that promised more trouble in the future. Alexandra shook her head as she looked at him.

"You won't let our uncle take him away, will you, Miss Lytton?" asked Jennifer as she scratched Rupert behind the ear.

"I will do my best," she replied, "but I must be honest. He is in charge here, and so of course he will have the final word about it."

The children's faces fell, and Isobel looked up from straightening Michael's pillows.

"I know that what Ned did was thoughtless, and that our uncle and Miss Wingate have every right to be angry, but I truly don't think he could help himself."

Alexandra looked at her inquiringly, and she continued.

"When our mother died and our neighbor, Mr. Wainwright, sold our property, he also sold our dog. He wouldn't let us bring Zach with us, and we didn't even get to say good-bye to him. It made all of us sad, but it broke Ned's heart. He cried himself to sleep every night for weeks. Zach used to sleep in Ned and Michael's room, beside their bed."

Alexandra nodded. The children seemed to have lost everything except each other, and having a dog did not seem to be too much to ask for. She intended to see to it that Ned got to keep his pup.

Browning did not see her enter the library. He had retired there in the hope of enjoying a few minutes of peace. After changing her gown and recruiting her strength with a cup of tea and the prospect of days of shopping in London, Pamela had retired to the morning room with her mother to plan their expedition and make their lists.

Ned and Rupert had retired upstairs with Miss Lytton, and even though Pamela had insisted that he immediately follow the governess, berate her, and remove the dog, he had had no desire to do so. The wave of anger that had swept over him at the desecration of his drawing room and Miss Lytton's defiance of him had passed as quickly as it had come, and he was ashamed that he had again lost control. He prided himself upon maintaining his composure and upon being just in his actions. It seemed to him he had managed to do neither.

Seeing the children, homeless and ragged and lost, had brought back uncomfortable memories of himself when he had first come to his grandmother at Greengage. He had struggled to put behind him all thought of his life before coming here, and now he had five very visible reminders under his very roof. He had loved Reeva devotedly and she had deserted him, and now she seemed to be playing upon his emotions even after her death. He had no wish to go upstairs and look at the children again.

Also, from a purely practical aspect, he did not wish to lose Miss Lytton's help and have to handle the children himself, nor did he want mud all over his immaculate jacket and breeches from the very active little dog. He had told Pamela that he would address the matter later—although the truth was that he didn't wish to address it all. He did not wish to be troubled by any of it. He had a larger problem to solve.

He had been reading Marcus Aurelius to restore his equanimity and had paused to close his eyes and focus on his personal talisman against distress—the orchards. When he opened his eyes, Miss Lytton was standing in front of him.

He straightened quickly and snapped his book shut. "Miss Lytton! I did not hear you come in," he said, quite unnecessarily.

"The door was ajar, so I let myself in. I'm sorry if I disturbed your reading of *Meditations*. I'm certain that you need it as an antidote to this morning's contretemps. I came to apologize for the destruction to your drawing room and to Miss Wingate's gown."

"You can scarcely be held accountable for those, Miss Lytton."

"I'm afraid that I can be, sir. I am responsible for the children, so I am responsible for their actions. And I wish to speak with you about Ned and the pup."

Briefly she recounted for him the story that Isobel had told her, and when she had finished, he nodded.

"He may keep the pup—but he must not, of course, bring it into the house in such a state again. Butterworth has hours of work to do to restore the drawing room."

Alexandra smiled. "I'm certain that you can count on Ned to do his best, Mr. Browning. Thank you for being so kind to him."

"I cannot see that you leave me any choice, Miss Lytton," he replied dryly. "I have never before encountered an angry hedgehog, but I have discovered that even an eagle must respect it."

Alexandra looked back at him, laughing. "I did not think you would remember that."

"I am beginning to think, ma'am, that I shall never forget it."

"Never fear, Mr. Browning. You will make a quick recovery from the spines of the hedgehog." Still laughing, she closed the door behind her.

He sat and smiled at the door for several minutes before returning to Marcus Aurelius. For the first time since the children's arrival, he felt hopeful about the future.

CHAPTER 12

Through the soft, cool stillness of the evening floated the song of a distant nightingale. Richard Browning stood on the terrace, surveying his domain and allowing some of its peace to flow over him and soothe him. When he looked out across the orchards, their blossoms tinted pink and gold by the sunset, he could pretend that everything was as it had been two nights earlier. His world was well ordered and calm; everything was as it should be.

But it was not. It was true that the drawing room had almost been returned to its former pristine glory, but the house itself was no longer quiet. It was filled with movement. He was aware that the children were trying to be unobtrusive, that they and Miss Lytton were doing their best to go quietly about their business, but it was impossible not to notice their footsteps on the stairs, their distant murmuring and light laughter, the occasional piercing bark from Rupert.

The children, except for Michael, had been away much of the day before, having gone to Shellingham for clothing and other necessaries. He had provided Miss Lytton enough money so that the children could purchase something for themselves as well. Isobel had chosen a set of bright combs for her dark hair; Clarissa, a book; Ned, a collar for Rupert; Jennifer, a diary of her own. For Michael they had chosen a book about fencing. Miss Lytton had told him all about their choices and the details of their excursion to Shellingham.

"You see, it shows you just how to do everything," Jennifer had said gravely, pointing out some of the illustrations to Alexandra.

"And Michael is interested in fencing?" she had asked, a little doubtful about the choice.

"Oh, yes!" Clarissa had exclaimed, and the others, even Ned, had nodded in agreement. "He loves stories of duels and swordplay. We used to make up plays ourselves, in the old days, and Michael always had a wooden sword and he always made us put in a swordfight."

Browning had smiled upon hearing that, and for a moment he remembered some of the few happy moments of his own childhood. He had possessed a fine sense of drama himself, and had learned to handle a sword well.

They had ended their day in Shellingham in a most satisfactory way, having ices at the local pastry cook's shop. The only blot on the day, Miss Lytton had told him, was the fact that Michael had had to remain at Greengage, but they had made it up to him with his book and a pastry to take the place of the ice he had missed.

"You were very kind to provide all of that for them, Mr. Browning," she had said approvingly, her blue eyes grave. "For a while today they were children again."

He had invited her to join them again for dinner that night but, to his relief, she had thanked him and refused, pleading weariness after so long a day. The children once again had supper trays in their rooms—or rather, in Michael's room—and she had joined them. He and Pamela and Mrs. Wingate had enjoyed a pleasant evening together, during which the ladies recounted their plans for London and for the ball.

The two had gotten an early start that morning, eager

to be about their business as soon as possible. Browning had been pleased to see that Pamela's mood seemed much more cheerful than it had been. The only sour note struck during their parting that morning had been when she had reminded him that he must begin to think of appropriate schools for the children to attend.

"For the sooner it is done, Richard, the sooner we can be at peace again," she had said brightly, smiling at him as she climbed into the carriage.

He did not want to think about such a thing yet, although he knew that he must do so soon. Being reminded of Reeva each day was too painful. And he had not yet told the children that half of Greengage was theirs. Somehow he could not bring himself to do that. Once he had said it, it would be true—and Greengage would no longer be entirely his own.

For the moment, though, it was. He stared into the distance at the orchards as though memorizing their every detail. He smiled to himself. There was no need to do so; he had memorized the scene before him long ago.

He walked to the edge of the terrace, and was startled to realize that he was not alone. Beyond the box hedge that marked this end of the terrace, a small figure perched on a stone bench, looking out at the orchards.

He waited a moment to see if the child was going to notice him, but she seemed absorbed in the scene before her.

"Hello. You are Jennifer, are you not?"

She looked up quickly, her dark eyes—Reeva's eyes—wide, and nodded.

"Are you certain that you won't get a chill?" he inquired. "Perhaps you should go in where it's warmer."

Jennifer shook her head. "After the sun sets," she said. "I want to see the orchards."

Browning stared at her for a moment. "The orchards?" he asked. "Is that why you've come out here?"

She nodded again, concentrating on the view before her. "I have wanted to see them for a long time," she told him, her voice serious.

"But how did you know about them, Jennifer?" he asked, sitting down next to her on the bench.

She picked up the red leather diary that had been lying next to her, out of Browning's sight. "Because of this," she said. "It is our grandmother's diary."

"Yes, I know," he replied, feeling his heart leap at the familiar sight. "I used to read it when I was young."

This was enough to win her attention, and she turned away from the orchards for a minute. "You used to read it, too?" she asked, inspecting him closely.

He nodded. "And I would imagine what Greengage Manor looked like, especially the plum trees when they were in bloom."

"She wrote about the orchards very often," nodded Jennifer. "And she made me want to come here." She looked back out at the orchards. "I don't know why she left. Mama said our grandmother left because she fell in love and ran away to a more exciting life. But she should have come back, I think, and brought you and Mama here—at least to visit."

"Yes, I think you are quite right," said Browning slowly. "I think she should have brought us here."

Jennifer turned to regard him seriously. "Then why didn't she?"

"I don't know. She never told me." He sat and stared ahead of him, for once not seeing the plum trees. "But I think, perhaps, that she was afraid to come home."

"Afraid?" Jennifer's voice was puzzled. "Why would she be afraid to come back to a place she loved so much?"

"Perhaps it was because she loved it so much that she

was afraid. Her father was very angry when she ran away, and she might have thought that he wouldn't let her come back here."

"Would he have let her, do you think?" Jennifer's voice was grave.

Browning thought about it for a minute. "I don't know," he admitted. "I know that he was very hurt and angry for a long time, because she was their only child. And he died just a few years after she ran away, but she didn't know it."

"Why didn't anyone tell her?"

"No one knew where she was. She didn't ever write to her parents, and then the revolution began in France, and it was hard to find anyone. Your mother and I were born in France, but after things got very bad there, we left and wandered from country to country."

Jennifer nodded wisely. "I know. Our grandfather was a traveling gambler—just like our father was."

"Yes. That is true." Browning could bring himself to say no more about that.

Jennifer had been thinking about the implications of the conversation. "But when her father died, was her mother all alone since there weren't any other children?"

"Yes, she was—and she was very lonely."

Jennifer turned and looked at him closely. "But you came back here, so then she wasn't lonely any more." She was making a simple statement of fact.

"That's right. When I came, she wasn't lonely any longer." Nor had he been lonely any longer, he thought, but he didn't add that.

Jennifer smiled at him. "I'm glad you came back and that she was happy."

Then she turned back to watch the orchards in the last lingering rays of the sunset. When nothing more could be seen of them through the thickening twilight,

Take a Trip Back to the
Romantic Regency Era
of the Early 1800's

4 FREE BOOKS ARE YOURS!

4 FREE
Zebra Regency Romances!
(A $19.96 VALUE!)

**Plus You'll Save Every Month With
Convenient Home Delivery!**

We'd Like to Invite You to Subscribe to Zebra's Regency Romance Book Club and Send You 4 Free Books as Your Introduction! (Worth $19.96!)

If you're a Regency lover, imagine the joy of getting 4 FREE Zebra Regency Romances and then the chance to have these lovely stories delivered to your home each month at the lowest price available! Well, that's our offer to you and here's how you benefit by becoming a Regency Romance subscriber:

- 4 FREE *Introductory Regency Romances are delivered to your doorstep (you only pay for shipping & handling)*
- *4 BRAND NEW Regencies are then delivered each month (usually before they're available in bookstores)*
- *Subscribers save almost $4.00 off the cover price every month*
- *You also receive a FREE monthly newsletter, which features author profiles, discounts, subscriber benefits, book previews and more*
- *There's no risks or obligations...in other words, you can cancel whenever you wish with no questions asked*

Join the thousands of readers who enjoy the savings and convenience offered to Regency Romance subscribers. After your initial introductory shipment, you'll receive 4 brand-new Zebra Regency Romances each month to examine for 10 days. Then, if you decide to keep the books, you pay the preferred subscriber's price, plus shipping and handling.

It's a no-lose proposition, so return the FREE BOOK CERTIFICATE today!

Say Yes to 4 Free Books!

Complete and return the order card to receive your FREE books, a $19.96 value!

A $19.96 value – **FREE** No obligation to buy anything – ever.
4 FREE BOOKS are waiting for you! Just mail in the certificate below!

FREE BOOK CERTIFICATE

YES! Please rush me 4 FREE Zebra Regency Romances (I only pay $1.99 for shipping and handling).I understand that each month thereafter I will be able to preview 4 brand-new Regency Romances FREE for 10 days. Then, if I should decide to keep them, I will pay the money-saving preferred subscriber's price for all 4... (that's a savings of 20% off the retail price), plus shipping and handling. I may return any shipment within 10 days and owe nothing, and I may cancel this subscription at any time.

Name _____

Address _____ Apt.____

City _____ State_____ Zip_____

Telephone (___) _____

Signature _____

(If under 18, parent or guardian must sign)

Offer limited to one per household and not to current subscribers. Terms, offer and prices subject to change. Orders subject to acceptance by Regency Romance Book Club. Offer Valid in the U.S. only.

RN084A

lll..l..lll...ll..ll..ll..ll..ll..ll..ll..lll..l

REGENCY ROMANCE BOOK CLUB
Zebra Home Subscription Service, Inc.
P.O. Box 5214
Clifton NJ 07015-5214

PLACE
STAMP
HERE

she slipped off the bench, said good night, and went up for her supper.

Browning sat for a long time in the darkness that evening, thinking about the past and about the quiet, tenderhearted child who looked so much like Reeva but who sounded so much like his grandmother.

CHAPTER 13

The next morning Alexandra rose early, long before the children would awaken, so that she could steal a few minutes of solitude. She quietly checked their rooms to make certain that all was well and smiled to see Rupert snuggled next to Ned, his furry muzzle and black nose just visible above the covers.

She strolled out of the house as she had on the first morning after their arrival. She paused and looked about carefully for Richard Browning, however. If she could see him, she had promised herself that she would either go back in immediately or walk in the opposite direction. Having already encountered him in the orchards at this time of morning, she had no desire to appear to be seeking a meeting. Seeing no sign of movement, she started in the direction of the orchards.

Walking down a green alley between two rows of trees, she stopped to look up through the blossoms at the lightening sky. By the end of summer, plums, plump and dusky, would hang heavily from the trees. She sighed to think she would not be here to see it. By then she would be in Yorkshire at her new post—but it would be a comfort to think of the Delacroix children living happily here at Greengage Manor.

She had had some doubts about their uncle when they first arrived, but he seemed to be handling the situation well after the initial shock. She did not allow herself to think about Miss Wingate.

How peculiar a circumstance it was, she mused, that the children's uncle should be her mysterious dancing partner. Remembering that delightful evening, she closed her eyes and began to hum, turning in the steps of a waltz.

With no warning, she was once again caught in a strong pair of arms that guided her through the steps. Her eyes flew open and she looked up once again into a pair of smiling eyes.

"Forgive me, Miss Lytton, but I heard you humming and I could not resist," he said.

"I believe that I have heard you say that before, sir," she replied, smiling up at him.

"But then I did not know your name, ma'am. If I had, I would have been able to find you after you abandoned me that night," he answered, pulling her closer.

"I didn't abandon you, Mr. Browning. My presence as a governess was requested, and I had to go immediately."

She swallowed briefly, for there was an unexpected tightening in her throat, then continued easily, "And since I am a governess, finding me again would have been an exercise in futility, as you know."

"I know no such thing." Browning's voice was abrupt. "So far as I know, governesses may dance at balls."

"Indeed they may, if they have their employer's permission," she conceded.

"And I wished to see you again. I tried for days to find out who you were."

Alexandra, thinking of Miss Wingate, turned the conversation. "Ah, but now you know my name, and you have seen me again—and now we have had our dance, sir." She slipped from his arms and started back toward the manor house.

"It is almost time for the children to wake, and so I

should return to them," she said cheerfully. "I shall leave you to have your morning walk in peace."

Browning, suddenly remembering Pamela as well, stood and watched her walk away. He was grateful that she was a sensible woman and had let the moment pass gracefully. He wondered, though, if it really would have mattered to him that she was a governess if he had found her again before meeting Pamela.

He suspected that it would not have mattered at all.

Browning found it difficult to concentrate that morning, and he found himself walking into the entrance hall and up the stairs rather more often than was necessary. He told himself that he was simply keeping an eye on the children, making certain that Ned and Rupert were not redecorating any of the rooms. He knew, however, that he was hoping to see Miss Lytton again. Finally, he gave up all pretense and went up to Michael's room on the third floor, certain that he would find her there with the children.

When he opened the door and walked in, everyone looked up in surprise. Among the children, only Jennifer and Ned had spoken with him, and all of them—except Jennifer, who rather liked him, and Michael, who feared no one—were uneasy in his presence. They had been laughing as he entered, but silence fell almost immediately and Ned hurried forward to catch Rupert before he could welcome the newcomer by leaping upon him.

"Good morning, Mr. Browning," said Alexandra with perfect composure. "We were about to play charades. Would you care to join us?"

"Ah—no, though I thank you for the invitation. Actually, I have come to extend an invitation of my own."

Everyone, even Rupert, looked up at him expectantly.

"I thought that perhaps you might like to join me in the greengage orchard for a picnic this afternoon."

"A picnic!" exclaimed Clarissa in delight. She loved picnics above all things except reading. If the others felt that they had picnicked quite enough during their journey, they were too polite to say so.

"But what about Michael?" asked Jennifer, who liked the idea of going to the orchard, but who couldn't again abandon her brother. He had missed the trip to Shellingham and the ices they had had there, and she didn't feel that a second outing without him would be fair. "We can't leave him here alone."

"Nor will we," Browning assured her, liking her loyalty. "The surgeon told me that Michael needs some fresh air. We'll put him in the pony cart and go to the orchard by a back lane."

"A pony cart?" He had Ned's full attention now. "May Rupert and I ride in it, too?"

Browning nodded. "If the ladies will not mind walking, I believe that we can pack the lunch, Michael, you, and Rupert in the cart. And, since Michael cannot yet use his arm, perhaps you will be good enough to drive it, Ned."

Ned's face glowed. "I get to take the ribbons!" It was clear that his cup had just run over.

Alexandra and Isobel were looking at Browning with some concern, but he smiled at them and added in a low voice, "Toby is a very elderly pony, and he seldom has the opportunity to pull a cart. He will enjoy the outing, and his pace will be gentle enough not to jar Michael."

The two ladies relaxed, their fears about Ned galloping away—or being galloped away with—allayed by his reassurance. As for Ned, he spent the next few hours regaling Rupert with tales of his driving prowess. The terrier, who had accepted Ned as his personal deity, listened with gratifying attention.

The weather conspired to make the picnic a gala

event. Bright sunshine filtered through the blossoms onto the grass where Browning and the ladies laid the cloth for their feast. After setting down the baskets that had been carefully filled by Mrs. Melling, they strolled to the end of the greengage orchard. A lane ran between it and the cherry orchard, and it was there that they would wait for the pony cart. In a few minutes Jennifer sighted it and they all waved. Ned was carefully holding the ribbons, although the pony moved so sedately that he needed no guidance whatsoever.

"There was a time when Toby would have trotted every inch of the way," Browning chuckled. "Now, however, he is satisfied with a slower pace. He knows every lane at Greengage by heart."

"Did your grandmother drive the pony cart here on the estate?" inquired Alexandra. In her experience, pony carts were for the young, like Ned.

Browning nodded. "That is the same pony cart that my mother drove, although she drove a different pony, of course. My grandmother always kept the pony cart for children who came to visit. Every neighbor child has driven it, and she would have loved to see Ned holding the ribbons."

He did not add that his grandmother had always hoped that her own grandchildren would one day ride in the cart, nor that when he had finally come, he had been too old for it. Ned, her great-grandson, was the first of her own family to use it.

"Do you think that I could learn to drive it?" asked Jennifer hesitantly. Isobel and Clarissa looked at her in surprise. Jennifer was usually quite timid and seldom talked to people she did not know well.

Browning nodded emphatically. "Of course you could. In fact, I daresay that Ned would be glad to show you how after our picnic." He felt perfectly secure in making

Ned the teacher, for he knew that Toby would do the teaching and would bring them safely back again.

After the occupants of the pony cart had descended, Toby was freed from his harness and given a carrot as a reward for his efforts. Browning, Alexandra, and Isobel carried the blanket and cushions that had been brought for Michael, and they made their way back to the baskets through a tunnel of fragrant white, where blossoms fell in the soft breeze like a scattering of snow. Ned and Clarissa, accompanied by Rupert, raced ahead, followed by Alexandra, Michael, and Isobel, who made their way more slowly. Last of all came Browning and Jennifer. To his surprise, she had fallen back from Michael's side to walk with him.

They didn't talk, both of them satisfied merely to be there and to look around them hungrily, as though they were afraid they would miss seeing something. The others arrived at the baskets, settled Michael on his blanket, and began unpacking the delights that Mrs. Melling had prepared for them.

As they neared the group, Jennifer looked up at her uncle. "I think this must be what heaven is like," she said gravely. "And it doesn't seem so cruel that Mama was taken from us if she has a place like this to love. Papa, too, of course," she added hastily, "though I don't know whether he would really like it so much."

Browning, who had had much the same thought about heaven, nodded in agreement. "And we are doubly lucky," he replied, "because we get to see this now."

She nodded, satisfied, and they sat down to the feast. Cold goose and turkey pie, cold meat and cheese, fruit, slices of bread and butter, a crock of plum jam, and— since Ned had already visited the kitchen and made a friend of Mrs. Melling—plum cake as well.

"I understand, Michael, that you're interested in

fencing." Browning had been studying the face of the young man seated across from him—a face that looked all too dearly familiar.

Michael's eyes lighted up and he nodded. He had been watching his uncle covertly, wondering when he would take him to task for his attempt at highway robbery. He assumed that Browning was biding his time until he thought his nephew in better health, and he had been waiting uneasily for that moment. Now, with the mention of fencing, he forgot that matter entirely.

"I've seen it done in plays, of course, but I've never seen anyone do it properly. Do you fence, sir?" he asked eagerly.

"Once upon a time," Browning admitted, "although I'm certainly rusty now. What you need is a proper instructor."

Michael fairly leaped from his cushion, his dark eyes shining. "Do you mean it, sir? That I could really learn?"

"I see no reason why you should not," replied Browning. And he did not. That was a provision for his nephew that he should be able to make easily enough, and it might give the boy a healthy outlet for his restless energy.

"Thank you, uncle," said Michael fervently, his mind already far away as he pictured himself, a practiced swordsman, doing battle in a hundred dashing situations—and winning always, of course. He eased back against his cushion and closed his eyes.

Browning nodded and sank back against a borrowed cushion. Above him a lazy bee hummed monotonously among the blossoms. Clarissa was reading, and Miss Lytton and Isobel had strolled back to the pony cart with Ned and Jennifer. He had planned to accompany them, but Ned had insisted that he knew how to harness Toby to the cart and Miss Lytton, standing behind him, had nodded. He was certain that if Ned could not do it, she could do so. The children could come to no harm rambling around the manor grounds with Toby.

He and Michael dozed gently in the late afternoon sun, awakening only when the others returned and Rupert pounced upon Browning before Ned could capture him. He awakened to a rough tongue licking the side of his face, and Ned scolding the pup for his lack of manners.

"I'm sorry, sir," he apologized as Browning opened his eyes.

He sat up quickly to protect himself from further terrier attacks and glanced about him. All traces of the picnic had been packed away, and Miss Lytton was gathering up Michael's blanket and cushions.

"Perhaps we should go before the sun slips lower and it grows too cool," she suggested. "We didn't wish to wake you, but Rupert has done that for us."

"Yes, very effectively," agreed Browning, eying Rupert with a wary eye. "Did you enjoy driving the pony cart?" he asked, turning to Jennifer.

Her eyes shone. "It was wonderful, uncle! I never felt so important or so free in all my life!"

"And she was good," volunteered Ned. "She wasn't afraid at all. She's going to ride back with Michael and me."

"May we go on another picnic tomorrow?" asked Jennifer.

"You may go on a picnic whenever you please," he assured her. "And when I return from London, I shall go with you."

Her face fell. "You're going away? How long will you be gone?"

"Not so very long," he assured her, looking speculatively at Miss Lytton as he considered an idea that had just occurred to him. "I must leave tomorrow, but I had thought perhaps all of you could join me there in a week, after Michael is well enough to travel."

The children stared at him. "London?" exclaimed Isobel. "Are you inviting us to London?"

"Perhaps you would enjoy a few days there." He smiled at them. "We could see the Royal Menagerie and go to Astley's to see the horses perform. And of course there would be the theater and shopping and the book stores."

By this time their eyes were alight with anticipation. Such delights were far removed from the world in which they had been living for too long. Then Browning paused a moment, and looked at Miss Lytton.

"I would need your help, naturally. This would mean extending your time with us, which I know is an imposition."

She looked at him reproachfully, for the children set upon her immediately, pleading with her to stay.

"We would like for you to remain even if we were staying here, Miss Lytton," said Clarissa. "Please, won't you stay with us for a few weeks?"

It was impossible for her to refuse, just as he had anticipated. Finally she gave way, laughing, and the children cheered and Rupert barked.

Browning smiled. Not only would he be giving the children a well-deserved holiday, but he would also be able to indicate to Pamela that she could not plan every moment of his day. He would see to it that he had some time for himself and he would, after all, have obligations to the children, too. She could not monopolize his every moment.

And Miss Lytton was, he thought, a very capable chaperon for them. She would keep things running smoothly so that he need not be overly concerned with their more mundane needs. And, upon occasion, he would naturally need to spend some time with the children—and with her.

For a brief moment he allowed himself to wonder just

where all this was leading. He had been avoiding the children who reminded him so sharply of his own childhood, yet he had spent the afternoon with them and now had invited them to London. He had a fiancée, and yet he was looking forward to Miss Lytton's company.

For the first time in many years, Richard Browning was falling prey to his emotions. His well-ordered life had become considerably livelier and he had no notion just where it all might be leading.

CHAPTER 14

"Do you think we'll get to go to Astley's again, Miss Lytton?" demanded Ned, as he and Rupert accompanied her up the stairs. "Do you think that I could ever be good enough to ride there someday? Which act did you like best?"

"Calm down, Ned," she told him, smiling at his excitement. "You'll work yourself into a frenzy."

The performances at Astley's Royal Amphitheater had transfixed him. Alexandra had never seen him remain still for so long. Indeed, the only reason that he could not have stayed there indefinitely was that Rupert had not been permitted to accompany them. His uncle, who had escorted them, had drawn the line at that.

Isobel, who was following them, laughed. "You know by now, Miss Lytton, that Ned *lives* in a frenzy. He wouldn't be normal if he were calm."

"You are right, of course," Alexandra agreed, as Ned and Rupert raced on ahead of them. "Did you enjoy the afternoon, too?"

"Of course," she replied, "although not as much as Ned, I must admit. What I am looking forward to most of all is the ball tonight."

Alexandra smiled. It had been pleasant to see Isobel gradually relax as she realized that the burden of taking care of her family no longer rested on her shoulders. A

dressmaker and a tailor had come to Greengage to measure the children for more suitable clothing since the
outfits that they had purchased in Shellingham had
been, their uncle informed them, only for use until they
could be properly attired. At his instructions, Isobel was
to have, among other items, a white ball gown, and he
had promised her that she would be permitted to come
to the ball he was giving to announce his engagement to
Pamela. Alexandra had been giving her dancing instructions for a week, and Isobel's eyes were bright with
excitement.

"Of course you are," she agreed. "How could it be
otherwise? Your first ball is always wonderful."

"Are you excited about going, Miss Lytton?"

"Naturally. There is nothing so lovely as a ball—the candlelight and the flowers and gowns and music." She did
not add that she had always seen them only as a bystander.

"Miss Wingate still doesn't think that I should be allowed to attend," confided Isobel. "She said that I am
not out yet—and that I probably never would be—but
Uncle insisted."

Alexandra smiled grimly. Miss Wingate had indeed
protested—and said all that she could that bordered upon
the insulting—but Browning had remained adamant. Isobel would be present for the entire evening and allowed to
dance, and all of the children would be allowed to come
down for a little while to watch the dancers and to enjoy
supper.

"And, Miss Lytton," he had said, turning to her at
the end of this lively discussion, "I should like for you
to remain for the entire evening as well."

"Of course she cannot!" said Pamela, her small face
flushing. "She is the children's governess and must
remain with them when they go upstairs."

"Nonsense! There will be a maid there should they need

anything, and they are quite old enough to put themselves to bed. Aside from that, she will be Isobel's chaperon, since you have been so concerned about her presence at the ball." He did not add that the Delacroix children had been quite old enough to take care of themselves for weeks on their long journey to Greengage.

Alexandra had curtsied and murmured her thanks for the invitation, grateful that she had a suitable gown with her since she had been to London for Alicia's wedding and the gala events before it.

All of the children, even Michael and Ned, were looking forward to the ball, and were pleased to be dressing in the fine clothes that had been made for them.

"There's to be an ice sculpture shaped like a great rose in the center of one of the tables at supper," announced Ned, who had already established his connections in the kitchen. "And there will be jellies and ices and macaroons and enough food for more than four hundred people!"

"They'd better not wait for you to go in to supper first, or there won't be enough for one hundred," observed his brother, grinning.

Ned accepted this compliment in the spirit it was offered, and leaned over to push Michael and pat Rupert. For Ned, the only drawback to the evening was that Rupert was not to be allowed to attend.

"But I shall bring you back something," Ned promised gravely, and Rupert wagged his stump of a tail in appreciation.

They were, Alexandra thought with considerable pride, a handsome group. A month ago they had looked like ragamuffins, lost and hopeless, but now they were well-dressed, well-groomed, and well-fed. Even Michael and Jennifer, the thinnest of them all, had begun to look healthy. Dark hair shining in the candlelight, the group descended the stairs together.

Guests had been arriving for some time and the dancing had already begun when they arrived in the ballroom. Alexandra had come down earlier in the evening to determine just where she and the children should be located. At one corner of the ballroom was a door opening into the billiard room. It was, she saw, screened by potted palms and a trellis of roses. The billiard room, she had decided, would be the perfect place for them. She and the girls could be seated behind the palms to watch, and the boys could entertain themselves with billiards. Even though Michael had not recovered enough to play, he had been giving Ned pointers on playing the game.

Alexandra, along with Jennifer and Clarissa, had settled themselves behind the palms, and Isobel had nervously entered the crush in the ballroom.

"What if no one asks me to dance, Miss Lytton?" she had asked anxiously.

Alexandra had looked at her and smiled. "Your card will soon be filled, my dear," she had assured her. Isobel looked radiant in her simple white gown. Browning had given her a string of pearls that glowed against her dusky throat, and a single white rose shone in her dark curls. "You look radiant."

Michael had grinned at her. "If I see that you're in a pinch, Belle, I shall come and rescue you. After all, I've learned the steps even if I can't use my arm very well yet."

All of the children, even Ned, had learned to dance while Alexandra was giving Isobel her lessons. The old schoolroom at Greengage, not used since their grandmother's time, had rung with laughter—and the encouraging barks of Rupert, who had done his best to snap at all of the available ankles as his contribution to the effort.

Alexandra's prediction proved correct, for Isobel had taken only a few steps beyond the palms when she was approached by a young gentleman, who bowed and extended his arm for her to take.

"Look! Belle has a partner!" Clarissa had been following her sister's movements carefully, and Michael and Ned came from the billiard room, cue in hand, to see for themselves.

A striking young man with golden hair that glistened in the candlelight had led her onto the floor. They watched in admiration as Belle moved gracefully through the figures of the dance.

"She hasn't missed a step," breathed Jennifer in relief. She had been watching her sister intently, fearful that something would go awry for Belle. "And she looks so happy, Miss Lytton. Just look at her face."

Isobel did indeed appear to glow as she looked up at the young man at the close of the dance and he bowed to her.

"Do you think that he will dance with her again?" asked Clarissa, watching closely.

"I shouldn't be at all surprised," replied Alexandra, "although a lady isn't supposed to dance with the same gentleman more than twice during the evening."

It was immediately obvious that Isobel would not lack for partners, for she was immediately encircled by a group of eager young gentlemen, all anxious to engage her for a dance. Alexandra rose from her place and made her way down the room to stand close to the group, watching carefully. She was pleased to see that Isobel had nothing of the flirt about her. Her manner was artless but charming, and she paid the young gentleman the compliment of listening to them as they prattled on.

As the orchestra began the next dance, a different young gentleman, this one a thin redhead with a merry face, led her onto the floor. If Isobel felt a pang at seeing her previous partner with another young lady, she showed no sign of it. Her attention was given entirely to her partner and to the other gentlemen that she encountered as she wove her way through the figures of the dance. Alexandra watched her approvingly.

Browning had escorted Miss Wingate onto the floor for this dance, and Alexandra glanced at them from time to time, not wishing to seem to stare. He danced as well as she remembered, and Miss Wingate looked very small and delicate—and golden—next to him. For a moment Alexandra thought regretfully of her own height. No one would ever look at her and think her engagingly fragile. Terrifyingly Amazon-like would be closer. Delightful, she thought to herself—a cross between an Amazon and a hedgehog. How irresistible!

Miss Wingate was elegantly attired, her gold ball gown heavily trimmed in broad bands of white lace, emphasizing her own golden, delicate beauty. Her diamond necklace glittered in the candlelight, as did her yellow ringlets. Alexandra could not help glancing down at her simple blue gown—and her only jewelry aside from gold earbobs was the gold locket she wore at her throat. Jealousy was not natural to her, but for just a moment she allowed herself to think that life was often unjust. Then she shook her head to clear it of such thoughts and turned her attention back to Isobel and to the two girls seated beside her, who were watching everything with large eyes.

Alexandra took the children in early to select their supper, and Ned was once again, as he had been at Astley's, transported. The array of culinary delights could have absorbed him for hours, but the others managed to move him along and to confine his choices to one plate, although Alexandra promised him one more opportunity after he had eaten his present selections. Appeased, he retired to the billiard room with the others.

"Well, I am relieved to see that you are not going to starve," said Browning, who had entered the room quietly and was surveying their loaded plates. Even Jennifer, he noticed, had a well-filled plate.

At that moment Isobel appeared, for she had promised Alexandra that she would have supper with them. It was, she felt, far safer for Belle to be with them during that time, for she would not be free to act as chaperon then. Michael rose and made a gallant bow to his sister, offering to bring her a plate, filled with the choicest delicacies, and a glass of lemonade, and Isobel sank gratefully onto a chair.

"It has been quite wonderful, Uncle. I do thank you for letting me attend, and for giving me the pearls and the lovely gown."

Browning, mimicking his nephew, swept her the same gallant bow. "It was my pleasure, Isobel."

Just then the orchestra began to play once more, this time a waltz. Browning turned to Alexandra and bowed once more.

"Miss Lytton, I believe that this is our dance," he informed her, offering her his arm and leading her to the door.

The children stared at one another and then, as one, rose to follow them. Together they stood behind the palms and watched their uncle sweep Miss Lytton onto the floor. As the couple whirled to the music, Browning looked down into her eyes, smiling. The children could see that they were talking, and suddenly their uncle threw back his head and laughed.

"He likes her," said Ned in wonder, leaving his cake for the moment untouched.

"I've never seen him laugh before," said Jennifer, her eyes wide.

"But look over there," whispered Clarissa, raising her eyebrows at a small figure in a gold gown standing to their right. "Not everyone is laughing."

The children looked. It was Miss Wingate, watching Browning and Miss Lytton, her small fists clenched, her chin jutting in anger.

The children looked at one another and chuckled. Life had not afforded them many pleasures until recently—but this appeared to be the choicest one thus far.

INTERLUDE

Alexandra's heart was thumping far too quickly as Richard Browning guided her onto the floor and took her firmly in his arms. Of necessity, she had been a practical woman all of her life, and she knew beyond a shadow of doubt that the man with whom she was dancing was not for her. Indeed, marriage with anyone was more than likely not for her. She would do her best to save part of her wages so that she could, when the time came, retire to some quiet village where she could live on very little—and possibly augment her funds by tutoring local children.

It was not an inspiring future, but she enjoyed her pupils and she was self-sufficient. She needed no one else. That, she had felt, must content her.

Dancing with Richard Browning threatened to overset all of that. She had always maintained a calm, easy manner. The only time she gave way to emotion was when anger overtook her at the mistreatment of someone else—usually children. Joy had been unknown to her—until tonight.

She had been delighted by their first dance, and it was a happy memory often relived, but tonight was different. Tonight he knew who she was and he had deliberately sought her out to waltz with her once more. What, she thought, could be the meaning of that—except that he took as much pleasure from her company as she found in his?

As they danced, the room turned into a kaleidoscope of shifting colors and lights. If he suddenly released her, she thought, she would go spinning across the room and be completely unable to regain her balance. The only thing upon which she could focus was his face. That became her anchor in the bright sea of music and gowns and laughter.

"What are you thinking, Miss Lytton?" The winged brows that she had found so remarkable when she first met him appeared to be taking flight as he looked down at her.

"I was thinking, sir, how astounding it is to be dancing with someone who is even taller than I," she remarked demurely. "And of how courageous you are to be dancing with someone who is a happy blend of the hedgehog and the Amazon."

Browning threw back his head and laughed. "Now that, Miss Lytton, is a formidable combination." As his laughter faded, he looked at her thoughtfully. "But then, I think you can be a most formidable lady."

Alexandra's heart sank. Having him consider her a formidable lady was scarcely lover-like. At the thought, she felt her cheeks turning scarlet. Where had her wits gone? Why was she expecting him to say something lover-like to her? *Hen-witted!* she scolded herself fiercely.

Browning was studying her face with interest. "I did not mean that you needed to show me just now how formidable you are," he said gently. "Have I said something to distress you?"

"Not at all," she replied easily, taking herself firmly under control. "How lovely an evening this is, Mr. Browning, and how kind you are to invite the children and me to enjoy it, too."

To her dismay, the strong arm around her waist, of which she had been so conscious, suddenly pulled her closer to him so that she could feel his warmth and smell the faint scent of bayberry. "I did not ask you to dance so that we could talk about the children, Miss Lytton."

His dark eyes searched her face, and she forced herself to take a deep breath before she spoke so that her voice would be even. She could not allow herself to betray how his words had affected her.

"Indeed?" she replied as lightly as she could. "And just why *did* you invite me to dance, sir?"

There was a brief silence. "Because I knew that dancing with you would give me pleasure, Miss Lytton. It was the sheerest self-indulgence."

Alexandra had no reply for this, but she felt her heart leap. He found pleasure in being with her! She smiled up at him.

"I must compliment you, Mr. Browning. You know precisely the proper thing to say to please your partner."

"You think that I am insincere?" he demanded.

She shook her head, still smiling. "No, I think that—" She stopped to measure her words carefully. "I think that saying the pleasant thing comes easily to you. You like those about you to be happy."

He stared at her, startled by her words. It was true, of course, but he had not realized his intent was so obvious. He did not like to live in the midst of emotional distress, but hearing her observation made him feel that he must often be less than honest in his dealings with others. That was not something he wished to think about just now.

"When we go back to Greengage, Miss Lytton, will you stay with us for a few weeks more? You have become vital to the children's happiness—and to mine."

Alexandra was caught between conflicting emotions.

He had just told her that she made him happy—but at the same time, he had asked her to stay on to take care of the children. How very convenient for him, said her practical self. He could compliment her and draw her in as easily as he would reel in a fish. She would not allow herself to be so blatantly manipulated.

"I would enjoy spending more time with the children," she replied, casting her eyes down demurely. "I have grown very fond of them."

She felt his hand tighten once more on her waist, and a wave of happiness crashed over her as she looked up once more into his smiling eyes.

CHAPTER 15

For the children, the ball was an unqualified success, the crowning moment of their trip to London. Seeing Miss Wingate discomfited had been a great delight to all of them, and they had regaled one another countless times with accounts of their uncle's dance with Miss Lytton and the reaction of their nemesis to it. None of this had been within Miss Lytton's hearing, of course.

"Miss Wingate looked like a kettle at full boil," said Clarissa gleefully.

Ned nodded seriously. "She looked as angry as the witch looked when she didn't get to cook Hansel and Gretel for her supper," he contributed. "Hansel and Gretel" had remained his favorite story—probably because of the house made of gingerbread, the others had decided.

"I wonder what Miss Wingate said to Uncle when she walked over to him after Miss Lytton left him," said Jennifer, who had watched the exchange closely. "She talked for ever so long and Uncle just listened. But his face went all hard."

"I daresay she was laying down the law to him," said Michael. "She certainly plans to rule the roost, but I can't imagine that our uncle will let her."

"I hope not," said Jennifer anxiously. "It will be awful for us if she does."

Clarissa nodded. "If she could, she would send us all back to America on the next ship that sailed."

They had no illusions about Miss Wingate. If their future were left in her hands, they knew it would be bleak.

"It is amazing that her cousin is so unlike her," observed Isobel dreamily. Her sisters and brothers had become accustomed to this topic of conversation after the ball, but they all glanced at one another when it surfaced yet again. "He is so kind—and such a gentleman."

Vincent Wingate was the golden gentleman who had danced with her first at the ball. He had dazzled her with his beauty and his attentiveness. As Alexandra had predicted, he had danced with her a second time that evening, and he had sent her white roses on the morning after the ball—her first flowers from a gentleman. He had written on the card: "More roses for your lovely hair." The others all knew what the card said because she had read it aloud to them and had left it on her dressing table, where she had reread it several times already and repeated it to them several times more.

Mr. Wingate had come to call on Isobel soon after the roses had arrived and Alexandra, very doubtful that she should be allowed to have a gentleman caller at all, had accompanied her to the drawing room.

"Ah, Miss Delacroix," he said, rising as she entered the room and bowing to her, "and Miss—" He hesitated as he looked at Alexandra, whom he had not met.

"This is Miss Lytton," said Isobel quickly. And he had bowed to Alexandra, but his eyes had remained on Isobel.

"How kind of you to call, Mr. Wingate," said Isobel, smiling at him as they seated themselves.

"How could you doubt that I would call?" he replied, his voice and manner just a little too warm for Alexandra's taste. Of course, she told herself, he could not know that Isobel was little more than a schoolgirl.

Doubtless Miss Wingate had told him as little as possible about the children.

"The roses that you sent are beautiful," she said, uncertain of how to reply to his question. "Thank you for thinking of me."

Alexandra watched him, knowing what would inevitably be said next.

"I could not do other than think of you, dear lady," he assured her. "And I hope to see one my roses worn in your hair as a mark of your favor—perhaps tonight at the rout given by the Fairfaxes? I know that Mr. Browning will be attending."

Isobel flushed painfully, and Alexandra interceded quickly so that she would not have to admit that, being only a child—and an interloper, at that—she had not been invited.

"Miss Delacroix and her brothers and sisters will be leaving for Greengage Manor tomorrow morning, so naturally they need their rest tonight."

Isobel had thrown her a grateful glance as Mr. Wingate had nodded.

"I am disappointed, of course, but I shall look forward to seeing you—both of you—again at the house party there."

He had stayed a few more minutes, making desultory conversation about the house party and his cousin's approaching marriage, then bowed and taken his leave, giving Isobel a last intense glance as he bowed over her hand. Alexandra and Isobel had gone back upstairs, Isobel floating on air because she had a gentleman admirer and Alexandra somewhat more earthbound for the same reason. At least, Alexandra congratulated herself, Isobel would be out of harm's way until the house party.

Alexandra had not allowed herself to think too much about her dance with Mr. Browning. He was, after all, her employer for the moment—and a man about to be married. He had, she knew, used her interest in him and her fondness for the children to convince her to stay on. After promising herself that she would not give way, she had done precisely that.

It was not so very dreadful, she told herself bracingly. She would be able to help the children for the time being and to earn a little more money for her retirement fund. She would still have time for a short holiday before her next post. She had agreed to stay until the wedding, which would take place shortly after the house party. After all, she was being practical, just as she had been all her life. And her emotions were firmly under control once more.

It was with considerable relief that she had gotten the children and Rupert into the carriage the second morning after the ball and set off for Greengage once more. Butterworth was following them with their baggage and a mountain of supplies for the house party. It would be interesting, she thought, to see just how Miss Wingate got on with the children this time. Surely she had had time enough to become accustomed to the notion that they were going to be a part of her life.

Miss Wingate, however, had done no such thing. As the others made their return trip to Greengage, she was attempting to force her fiancé to see reason.

"After all, Richard," she said pointedly, "you can have nothing but trouble so long as you allow those five children to remain under your roof. Not only must you keep a governess, but you must also deal with all of the other annoyances that children cause—like that messy little dog that created such havoc."

Browning almost smiled at the memory, for he had grown quite fond of Rupert, but he fortunately caught himself in time.

"But, as you have pointed out, my dear, sending them to school just now would be quite an expense."

The expense was not a problem, except in Pamela's eyes, but he thought it a card worth playing. Miss Lytton had told him that the children should be allowed an opportunity to adjust to their new home—and the fact that they had a home—before making any other changes in their lives. She would not be available to be their governess, of course, but she had suggested that he employ one and provide a tutor for Michael. Naturally, he could not mention that the advice was Miss Lytton's, for that would mean that Pamela would disagree with it immediately.

He cleared his throat. "It seems to me, my dear, that the best course for the moment would be to find a governess and a tutor who can prepare them for school so that they can stay at Greengage until they have recovered from their experiences during the past year."

She looked at him in disbelief. "Stay at Greengage? Have you gone quite mad, Richard? You are expecting a bride to take up the care of five children?"

"Of course I'm not, Pamela. You need not trouble yourself about them. They will be very well cared for by those I employ." He paused, thinking it over. "Of course, Isobel will have her coming out next year, and she would benefit from your help when that time comes."

"Isobel have a coming out?" she demanded incredulously. "Whatever are you thinking about? That would mean that the others must have the same, and the expense will become enormous! And that is not to mention the trouble that it will be to us!"

Browning was growing somewhat weary of the discussion of money, but he decided not to allude to it just now. Instead, he addressed himself to the important issue.

"Naturally Isobel must have a coming-out—and an appropriate dowry, of course." He decided that he might as well make that point now, but it drew, as he knew it would, another cry of anguish from his fiancée.

"How completely unnecessary, Richard! The next thing I know you will be saying that they will have some control over Greengage when they come of age!"

Browning swallowed somewhat convulsively, for this was a tender point. The house in Mayfair was his entirely, as was the majority of his grandmother's fortune, but Greengage was evenly divided between Richard and Reeva, and a modest bequest had been left to her.

He forced himself to nod. "That must be the way it is," he answered coolly.

"Do you not see, Richard?" Pamela said, making her voice patient and coaxing. "You need not do that at all. They don't know that they have inherited a half interest in Greengage, for you haven't yet told them. Have you?"

He shook his head. She knew just where to find his weakness.

"Then why should you tell them?" she asked simply.

"Because it is the proper thing to do," he responded, not meeting her eyes.

She shrugged. "You are going to be spending your money to take care of them. I would call it a fair exchange. You do that—pay for their schooling and their clothing—and you keep Greengage for us."

She slipped her arms around him. "After all, dear Richard," she said, returning to the honeyed tones of their courtship, "if they are safely out of the way, just think how very peaceful and pleasant our lives will be."

Unwillingly, he found himself listening to her, and he folded her in his arms and she allowed him to kiss her.

Pamela smiled. It was all so very easy when you knew how to manage men.

CHAPTER 16

Alexandra was grateful to arrive back at Greengage Manor. Even though she had stayed there a relatively short time, arriving there felt like coming home. The children, too, seemed to breathe a sigh of relief to be back on familiar ground, although she knew that they had enjoyed London. Isobel had stared soulfully out the window during the majority of the journey, and Alexandra felt a little uneasy about her obvious fascination with Vincent Wingate. Still, as she had reminded herself innumerable times, it was only natural that Belle would be drawn to the first handsome man who paid her such delightful compliments.

Rupert sprang from Ned's arms as they entered the hall and proceeded to race madly in figure eights through the adjoining rooms, leaping over footstools and low tables. Only when the pup ran out of breath was Ned able to recapture him. Even Rupert, it appeared, was glad to be home.

They settled comfortably into an easy routine. Alexandra was not really trying to teach them; she was merely trying to make them familiar with life in England and, in particular, life at Greengage. They enthusiastically resumed their dancing classes, and they learned the appropriate manners for a formal dinner. They dressed carefully and dined downstairs with Butterworth and the footmen to serve them. Alexandra had spoken with Browning about doing so, and he had considered it an excellent notion. Since Rupert was also learning appropriate social behavior, he came to the dining room with them and sat quietly in his basket, waiting for the bone that would come his way as a reward.

To their surprise, Richard Browning arrived on their fourth evening, just in time to sit down to dinner with them.

"We had not expected you to arrive for several more days, Uncle," remarked Jennifer, whose eyes had lighted up at his entrance. "The house party does not begin for another four days, does it?"

He nodded. "Miss Wingate will arrive one day before that, and the guests will arrive on the fourth day. However, there are a number of things I need to see to before their arrival."

If their faces fell at the mention of Miss Wingate, he chose not to notice that, and instead turned the conversation to them and their activities.

"Have you and Jennifer taken the pony cart out, Ned?" he inquired, looking at the boy's polished face.

Ned nodded vigorously. "And we've both driven it. Rupert's gone with us, too."

At this unexpected mention of his name, Rupert responded with a brief but imperative bark to call attention to his presence.

Ned turned and looked at him reprovingly. "No bone unless you're good, Rupert," he reminded the pup, who cast his eyes at the ceiling as though requesting heavenly strength.

"Is Rupert also receiving social training?" he inquired, glancing down the table at Alexandra.

She nodded. "We thought it would be a good idea, since Rupert is most certainly a part of the household."

Browning turned to Butterworth, who was just pouring his master a glass of claret. "And what do you think of having Rupert in the dining room, Butterworth?"

The elderly butler glanced at the pup and his anxious owner with a tolerant eye. "He is doing quite well, sir. I daresay he may earn two bones tonight."

Rupert, who had sat upright upon hearing his name mentioned again, wagged his abbreviated tail vigorously but restrained himself from uttering even a single bark, having caught Ned's worried glance.

Browning smiled. "If you have earned Butterworth's approval, there can be no question that you have mine."

Ned heaved a sigh of relief and returned to the serious matter of dining, and Rupert echoed his sigh, settling himself in his basket to await the bones, his chin hung over the edge of it and his gaze intent.

"And, Michael, how is your shoulder?" Browning inquired, turning to his other nephew and trying not to notice how very familiar his face looked.

"Mr. Davis thinks that in a few weeks I will be able to handle a sword nicely," Michael replied, smiling at the very thought of being able to achieve his dream of becoming an expert swordsman.

"And so you shall," his uncle assured him. "In the meantime, I am to go out hunting tomorrow with Gregg, my keeper, and you might wish to come along to see how it's done."

Michael's eyes lit up, and Alexandra watched with interest. He would not be able to shoot, of course, but just being allowed to go along was, she thought, an important step in establishing a relationship between uncle and nephew.

It was, she thought, going much better than she ever would have expected. Richard Browning appeared to be accepting his nieces and nephews as his family, and they

were certainly in need of that security. She was pleased—
but a little puzzled—by his acceptance of the children.
Particularly, she thought, since Miss Wingate's attitude
toward them was quite different from his own. She wondered, too, what had caused his intense anger at their
arrival. It did not really matter, she told herself, so long
as he had been able to change his feeling toward them.

At Jennifer's request, they had enjoyed several picnics
since their return. On the day after his return, they ad-
journed to the greengage orchard for yet another one.
Michael had accompanied Browning and Gregg that
morning and was full of their activities.

"Uncle showed me how to hold the gun, though he
wouldn't let me shoot it since the vibration would be too
hard on my shoulder. And he taught me some of the
safety rules for when we truly do go hunting."

"But you didn't actually shoot anything, did you?"
asked Jennifer, who disliked seeing any living creature
harmed.

Michael shook his head regretfully. "We saw some
pheasant, but they're not in season, of course. Rooks are,
though," he said, brightening, "but only for a day or two
more and we didn't see any today."

Jennifer gave a sigh of relief and returned her attention
to her slice of bread and butter.

"I wish I could learn to shoot," said Ned enviously.

"You will learn soon enough," Browning assured him.
"And Gregg will teach you both how to clean and care
for a gun properly."

"You have a good many guns and swords on the walls
of the library," observed Clarissa, who had inspected that
room's contents carefully, delighted to once more have
access to books. "Do you collect them?"

"I have purchased a few of them, but most belonged

to my grandfather. He was an excellent shot and loved to go hunting."

"Did he ever fight a duel?" inquired Clarissa curiously. Her latest novel involved such an event, and she was always eager for information.

"I believe he may have done so," replied Browning, frowning slightly.

Ned's eyes opened wide. "A duel? Did he kill his man?" he demanded.

"I really don't know the details of it," he responded briefly, turning his gaze to the trees. "It happened long before I came here."

"What about our mother?" said Clarissa. "Do tell us a little about what the two of you did when you were our age, Uncle. We know a few stories, but not many."

"I prefer not to remember the past," he said, his face growing closed.

To their dismay, Browning rose abruptly and walked away from them, down the green alley between the rows of trees.

"I didn't mean to upset him," said Clarissa unhappily. "I just wanted to know."

"Don't let it trouble you at all," replied Alexandra quickly. "Sometimes the past is unhappy and people don't wish to think about it." Inwardly, however, she was upbraiding Browning. Surely a grown man could control himself more effectively.

"Shall we go down to the pond and see the ducklings?" she said cheerfully, anxious to turn their thoughts to something else.

There was an eager assent to this, for all of the children, even Michael and Isobel, had been delighted to watch the antics of the new brood of ducklings that had just hatched. Ned and Rupert had seen them first, of course—although fortunately Rupert was kept distant from the mud, so he hadn't had the opportunity to inspect the new arrivals as closely as he wished. Ned had brought the news home and all of them had trooped down to see them.

"I will gather up the cloth and the basket and take them back to the house," said Alexandra. "Ned, you and Jennifer take the cart and the others will follow you over. I'll be down to join you in a few minutes."

The younger ones ran to Toby to hitch him to the cart, while the others strolled after them, Clarissa still casting uneasy glances toward their uncle. Alexandra tidied the remains of their picnic and, as soon as the children were out of view, walked purposefully toward Richard Browning.

He glanced up at the sound of her approach and managed a rueful smile. "Well, Miss Lytton, I see that I am in imminent peril from a hedgehog attack."

She did not return his smile. "That really was most uncalled for, Mr. Browning. Clarissa is distressed because she believes she upset you."

"Well, so she did," he replied, his smile fading as he turned away from her.

Alexandra, growing more annoyed, walked around so that she could face him once more. "She is a child, sir—a child who has lost her mother and her home. Even if she upset you, you are a grown man and fully capable of turning the conversation in a way that will not hurt her."

"Did you speak to your other employers in such a fashion, Miss Lytton?" he inquired, his gaze cold as he held back memories of loss and pain.

"Very seldom has it been necessary to do so, Mr. Browning, but I do not mind speaking the truth when it concerns the welfare of a child." Her gaze and her voice were as cold as his own.

"If that is the case, how much trouble you must have

caused. Perhaps that explains why you are now between posts."

He heard himself speaking as though he were listening to a stranger, and he cringed inwardly. He had lashed out at Clarissa because she had reminded him of times he did not wish to remember, and now he was attempting to punish Miss Lytton for calling that to his attention. He thought of his grandmother and how she had welcomed him to Greengage and helped him to build a new life. He could scarcely stand himself.

"I would remind you, sir, that I remained here as a favor to you—or, more accurately, as a kindness to the children so that they would feel that they had someone they could rely on. If you are suggesting that I leave, I shall do so immediately, after I have spoken with them."

She turned and started toward the basket, fully prepared to return to the manor house and pack. Before she could take two steps, however, regret for his hasty words overcame him. He caught her by the arm and turned her toward him.

"Forgive me for being such a boor, Miss Lytton." His voice and his eyes indicated the sincerity of his words, but Alexandra was not to be won over so easily.

"I am a paid employee, so you are entitled to speak to me as you wish—although I have no intention of continuing to be treated in such a manner—but you are not entitled to speak to the children in such a way."

She pulled away from him and continued, her voice stiff. "That is, I know that you are entitled to do so by law, but I had thought you a man of conscience and some sensitivity. Perhaps I was wrong."

When she turned to walk away again, he caught her around the waist and turned her to him, looking down into her eyes.

"Perhaps you were wrong, ma'am, but I assure you

that I am trying. I apologize abjectly, Miss Lytton. I know that I have a duty to the children and I know that I should not have spoken to you in such a manner when you are indeed doing me a kindness by remaining here."

He paused and watched her face for some sign of forgiveness. "Will you forgive me if I apologize to Clarissa?"

Alexandra nodded, holding herself as far away from him as she could and turning her eyes away from his. Relaxing was impossible when he stood so close to her, but she could hear the genuine regret in his voice and she thawed slightly.

"I shall make it up to all of you this very afternoon," he announced firmly. "There is a May fair in Shellingham, and we shall all go to see it."

Alexandra's eyes brightened. "The children would love it! And they would love going with you!"

Browning smiled, pulling her closer so that she was once again aware of the fragrance of bayberry, blending with that of the blossoms and newly mown grass. It was a heady scent, and she felt herself yielding.

"And what of you, Miss Lytton?" he asked, his breath warm upon her cheek. "Would you love to go with me?"

Alexandra caught herself just in time and slipped out of his arms. "Naturally I shall love going to the fair with you and the children."

Her voice was bright and she hurried to collect the basket. More than one governess had found herself in trouble for forgetting the line between herself and her employer. She did not plan to be such a one.

"I will tell the children and we will be ready shortly, sir." She called to him over her shoulder as she hurried toward the manor, eager to put as much distance as possible between them.

Browning stood and watched her go, the skirt of her red gown moving gently in the spring breeze. He shook his head to clear it. Once again he told himself that he was most fortunate that Miss Lytton was a sensible woman, and once again he wondered what had happened to the self-control upon which he had prided himself for so long.

Do what he might, he could not seem to escape the shadow of the past but somehow, he thought, he must surely make his peace with it.

CHAPTER 17

The ride to the fair was idyllic and Alexandra gave herself up to the pleasure of the afternoon. She and the children rode in the barouche while Browning followed them on horseback, riding next to them where the road was wide enough to permit it. The sun shone warmly on the hawthorn that lined the road, hedgerows white with blossom and starred with dog roses.

The fields north of Shellingham were thick with people who had come to the fair, and they could hear the sounds of merriment before they could see the crowds. By the time the fair came within view, Ned had almost fallen out of the open carriage because he was standing to crane his neck in that direction. Rupert was not with them because Browning had pointed out that so likely looking a terrier might be stolen in such a mob. Ned did not believe in taking chances with a prize like Rupert.

The coachman remained with the carriage and Browning's horse, and the group strolled off into the crowd of merrymakers. They almost did not make it past the cheapjack's booth, where that gentleman was entertaining passersby with a quick and amusing patter about the watch chains and pocketknives he had for sale. Ned was finally pried away from this interesting individual by the purchase of a small pocketknife, which he reverently tucked deep into his jacket pocket where it could not be lost.

The girls—and even Alexandra—found it equally difficult to pass quickly by a booth displaying ribbons of every sunset hue, from coquelicot to saffron. Once again they were able to move along only after small but interesting purchases were made. A swing, hung from the high branch of an oak, its ropes decorated with ribbons, was the next diversion. Each of them except Browning and Michael took a turn in it and, since Michael could not use his arm for pushing it, Browning was elected to do the work while Michael wandered off to inspect some of the other amusements.

After Ned and all of the girls had had their turn on the swing, Browning turned to Alexandra.

"Miss Lytton?" And he held the swing out for her to be seated.

"Oh, no, I'm not going to take a turn!" she protested.

"Please, Miss Lytton, try it!" urged Isobel, her encouragement echoed by Clarissa and Jennifer. "It's perfectly splendid. Uncle sends you high enough that you have a bird's-eye view of this part of the fair."

Seeing no way to escape gracefully, Alexandra seated herself. She had not been on a swing since her girlhood, and the experience was exhilarating. She discovered that the girls were right and she did have a wonderful view of the movement and color of the fair.

"Do you see anything exciting, Miss Lytton?" called Browning as he pushed her even higher.

Her eyes wandered over the bright scene before her, and suddenly she discovered that she did indeed see something more exciting than she had anticipated. In the distance was a great balloon of scarlet and white, clearly about to lift off and sail away. Climbing into the basket was a boy in a blue jacket, his dark hair shining in the sunshine. As he turned and waved to the crowd that had gathered, Alexandra could see that it was Ned.

She called the news to Browning and the girls, urging them to run and remove Ned before the balloon could lift off. Once they understood, they hurried away, leaving her to try to slow the swing by dragging her foot in the grass when its movement began to slow. Finally, almost falling off the seat, she leaped to the grass and started to run. Just as she did so, however, a great cheer went up from the crowd and the balloon rose into the sky. And there was Ned, waving vigorously as he peered over the edge of the basket.

She made her way as quickly as she could through the crowd until she saw Browning and the girls in the distance, all of them watching the progress of the balloon.

"Where is it supposed to set down?" she asked when she arrived next to them.

"No one seems to be quite clear about that," replied Browning grimly. "I'm going to get my horse and try to follow it until it lands. If you will be so good as to stay here with the others, Miss Lytton, Ned and I will rejoin you. If we are not back by late afternoon, just go directly home and we will meet you there."

"I'm glad that I'm not Ned," observed Clarissa as he went striding away. He had indeed apologized to her for being short with her, but all of the children were becoming keenly aware of how quickly he could lose his temper.

They stood there and watched until the balloon floated out of sight. Then Alexandra sighed and said, "Well, I suggest that we enjoy ourselves. There is nothing we can do about Ned just now, and I'm certain that your uncle will gather him up safely." She tried not to think about Ned's restless energy confined to the area of the basket. He was an intelligent boy and so he would surely see the necessity of staying still.

She glanced at the girls. "Where is Michael?" she asked.

In all the excitement, she hadn't realized that he was not with them.

No one knew, nor had anyone seen him since they had first started to swing.

"At least we know he's not in the balloon," observed Clarissa. "And we can find him before Uncle comes back."

"Or at least we hope we can," replied Isobel, whose experiences with Michael made her less positive.

As they threaded their way through the throng, Clarissa sighted a tent where a play was being presented. The playbill showed two swordsmen engaged in a duel, and so they paid for their tickets and entered, certain that they would find him in the audience. The play was in progress, so they seated themselves quietly on a bench in the back and waited for their eyes to adjust to the relative darkness.

A careful scrutiny of the backs of countless heads finally convinced them that Michael was not within the tent, and they departed, with Clarissa looking regretfully over her shoulder at the players and the dramatic scene taking place on the stage. Robin Hood had just entered, long bow in hand, and was taking careful aim at the Sheriff's man, who was holding Maid Marian captive.

"Do you think we can come back and see it all the way through?" she begged as they made their way into the sunlight. "They'll be presenting it once more this afternoon."

"Perhaps if we find Michael in time," murmured Alexandra and Clarissa groaned.

After they had made their way past a magic show, a rope dancer, and a wrestling match with no sign of the wanderer, Alexandra turned to the girls once more.

"Does anyone have an idea about what else would appeal to Michael?" she asked the girls.

Jennifer nodded hesitantly. "Is there a place where he could make a wager?" she asked in a low voice.

"Do you mean a place where he could gamble?"

"Yes," she replied, her voice lower still. Alexandra looked at the other girls and they reluctantly nodded their heads in agreement.

"If that's the case, then we'd certainly better find him before your uncle returns," Alexandra said grimly.

An intensive search turned up a cockfight, and Alexandra told the girls to wait for her outside. Most unwillingly she entered the tent, where a makeshift ring had been established for the matches. A new one was just beginning, and a fresh, beady-eyed cock had just been placed in the ring to face the bloodied champion of the previous fight. The enclosed area smelled of sweat and sour ale and blood. Alexandra held her handkerchief to her nose as she glanced about the men gathered to watch the bloodletting. To her relief, there was again no sign of Michael, and she made a hasty exit, not noting a man who had been staring at her and who slipped quietly out of the tent after her.

Jennifer tugged at her sleeve and Alexandra bent down to hear what the child was saying. "Perhaps if you found a place that has faro. Michael is fond of card games," she whispered. "And he's really quite good. Our father taught him."

Splendid, thought Alexandra. A junior gamester. His uncle would be delighted by this news—particularly when placed cheek by jowl with Michael's attempt at highway robbery.

"Very well," she said aloud, smiling at Jennifer and patting her on the shoulder. "Let us see what we can find."

It did not take long. Very soon they discovered a tent that offered faro and hazard, accompanied by strong punch, and there they discovered Michael. He had won a fair amount of money and consumed far too much punch, so he was disposed to linger at the tables. A word or two from Alexandra seemed to have a sobering effect, however, and he soon rejoined his sisters outside.

"We are going to find somewhere to eat," announced Alexandra grimly. Not only were they hungry, but she also judged it necessary to balance the punch Michael had consumed with something more substantial. When they saw tables set out under a tree and two pigs being roasted in a pit, they stopped to dine.

Dinner was much better than she had expected, and as they ate Michael's head appeared to clear and he glanced around the table.

"Where's Ned?" he asked suddenly.

"Gone," said Isobel briefly.

"What do you mean, 'Gone'?" he inquired. "Gone where?"

"In a balloon," replied Clarissa. "It sailed off in that direction." And she pointed to the north.

Michael stood up quickly and then, feeling the effects of the punch, sat back down just as swiftly. "We must do something to help Ned!" he announced.

Isobel looked at him with disgust. "You've already done something," she observed tartly. "You went off to gamble and drink and left the rest of us."

Michael flushed, and Jennifer, unable to stay upset with him, said reassuringly, "Uncle has gone to find him. He can do that better than any of the rest of us."

Her brother flushed even more deeply at that and stared down into his plate. "I suppose I haven't been much good at taking care of any of you," he said in a low voice.

"Oh, I don't know," said Isobel mercilessly. "You've committed highway robbery, gotten yourself shot, and now gone off by yourself and forgotten the rest of us."

Michael sat staring at his plate, not meeting anyone's eyes, and Alexandra glanced at Isobel's angry face. She could not bring herself to reprove the girl, though, for she had been the one who had to bear the brunt of the responsibility for her sisters and brothers during the past year. It was abundantly clear that Michael's notions of helping were far more likely to complicate matters.

"We still have a little more time before we must start for Greengage," she said briskly, hoping to divert everyone's thoughts, for Clarissa and Jennifer were looking just as upset as the other two. "Now that we've eaten, let's take a look at the booths we've missed."

Silently the others rose and joined her, but conversation was nonexistent. Alexandra paused in front of a Punch and Judy show, hoping that they would be amused, but the only comment she heard was Michael's.

"Sounds just like home," he observed bitterly, and Alexandra wondered if he was referring to the exchange between him and his sister or if he was referring to the relationship between his parents. The girls made no comment, and after a while all of them walked to the next booth.

Even though they had just eaten, Alexandra purchased gingerbread for all of them, operating on the belief that eating something that smelled wonderful would make everyone feel better. And, strangely enough, it seemed to do so. Even Jennifer, who took only a bite of hers and walked along holding it close to her nose, was smiling.

They passed a booth that was selling playing cards and Isobel turned to Michael. "Perhaps we should see if they have a deck with six aces, Michael. If they do, I'll buy it for you."

Her tone was tart, but she was smiling, and Michael grinned back. "I've told you and told you, dear sister, that I have no need of extra aces. I can win with an ordinary deck and no fudging."

Isobel sniffed and they continued along until they

heard a cry from Jennifer. They all wheeled back toward where she was standing, thinking that something dreadful had occurred. Alexandra was the first to reach her side.

"Isn't he wonderful, Miss Lytton?" she asked breathlessly. "May I have him?"

All of them drew close to the booth where Jennifer was standing. On the counter was a cage containing a dormouse, staring at Jennifer with wide eyes and sniffing her hand inquisitively.

"Oh, please, Miss Lytton. He isn't any larger than a teacup and I'd take such good care of him. Ned has Rupert, so do please let me have Will!"

"Will?" asked Michael, his winged brows rising. "You've already named the creature and you named the poor thing Will?"

Jennifer nodded energetically. "After Shakespeare!" she replied. "When you do his plays now, Michael, and act out the scenes, Will can be there to watch you!"

"I am speechless," he replied. "I can see myself on-stage, looking out in the audience at the first row, and there, watching intently, whiskers quivering, is—Will!" He turned to Alexandra. "I don't see how you can say no to her, Miss Lytton. It appears to me that Will has already become a part of the family."

Alexandra laughed. "I'm afraid that you're right, Michael. Jennifer has set her heart upon him." She did not add that Jennifer had set her heart upon very few things. The others knew that well enough. Smiling at the girl's happy face, she paid for Will without a second thought. Mr. Browning and Miss Wingate would have to adjust to life with a terrier *and* a dormouse.

As they walked back to the barouche in the gathering twilight, a horseman approached them and waved. To their relief, they saw that it was Browning, with Ned riding behind him.

"Ned!" cried Isobel, running toward them. "Are you hurt?"

"Far from hurt," responded her uncle as he dismounted and Ned slipped from the horse's back. "He is in much better condition that the man operating the balloon."

"Mario is a great gun!" exclaimed Ned. "You've never seen such a thing in your life as how everything looks from up in the sky! Like a giant patchwork quilt!"

He looked blissfully at Isobel. "I want to have a balloon of my own so that I can fly whenever I want to!" he announced.

As the children climbed into the barouche, Alexandra said to Browning in a low voice, "I see that he is riddled by regret for taking the ride without permission."

Browning glanced at her and almost smiled—but not quite, for the afternoon had taken a heavy toll on his patience. "As you see, ma'am, he is overcome by remorse. I daresay it will take him weeks to recover. I know it will take me that long."

"You should have been there, Michael!" exclaimed his little brother, and his chest puffed out importantly. "Mario said that I did splendidly!"

"I believe his words were that he'd never seen anything quite like you," observed Browning dryly, and the others laughed.

"It's amazing that the poor fellow could talk at all after being trapped in a tiny basket with Ned for an hour or two," said Michael.

Ned gathered his tattered shreds of dignity and turned to Jennifer, focusing for the first time on the cage she was carrying.

"What do you have there, Jenny?" he inquired, lowering his face to a level with Will's.

"A dormouse!" she announced proudly. "His name is Will and he's going to live in my room."

"He looks like a very small squirrel. Rupert will love him!" exclaimed Ned enthusiastically. "They will be able to play together and have a splendid time."

The others glanced at one another and Browning winced. "I don't believe that the dormouse would appreciate close contact with Rupert," he said. "In fact, Rupert might be disposed to feel that your pet is fair game."

Jennifer looked at her uncle, horrified. "Do you mean that Rupert might try to eat Will?" she demanded.

Her uncle nodded. "Terriers are ratters, so Rupert might very well try to go after—Will." He had to think for a moment before coming up with her pet's name. "So it would be wise to keep Will in his cage and to keep it up high enough that Rupert can't get to him."

Jennifer clutched the cage more closely to her, but Ned shook his head with determination. "Will is a part of our family now since Jenny's chosen him, and Rupert will just have to learn that."

Browning groaned softly and tried not to think of what excitement might lie ahead of him and his household as the two pets grew accustomed to one another.

As they rode home through the late spring evening, no one—not even the coachman or Browning—noticed the lone horseman following them at a careful distance.

CHAPTER 18

The remaining two days before Pamela Wingate's arrival were relatively peaceful. It was true that the household was in a constant bustle as Butterworth and Mrs. Melling supervised their staff in preparations for the house party, but it was a cheerful, purposeful bustle. A wing of the house seldom used had been thrown open once more and the guest chambers aired and cleaned and polished. The baking had been extensive and fragrant, so Ned had paid countless visits to the kitchen to inspect and sample the results. It amazed Alexandra that there were no complaints about his constant invasions, usually assisted by Rupert, but it was plain that he had become a favorite. Indeed, the staff appeared to enjoy all of the children—as well as Rupert and the newly arrived Will, who had been introduced to them by traveling in Jennifer's pocket.

Richard Browning, on the other hand, was having a little more difficulty adjusting to the household bustle. The thought of having Miss Lytton leave after the house party was decidedly unsettling. She had a calming effect upon the children and their menagerie—or perhaps upon him, helping him to deal with the situations that had arisen because of their presence more reasonably than he might otherwise have done. At any rate, he did not like to think of her leaving—entirely because of her helpfulness with the children, as he was quick to remind himself.

In fact, the more he thought of the matter, the less certain he was that he could deal with the children properly once she was gone, even with the help of a new governess and a tutor. It was possible that Pamela was right. The best thing for them all would be to send the children away to school and have them spend holidays at Greengage. Jennifer was the only one with whom he felt he had established a slight rapport, and he felt a twinge of guilt for considering sending her away from a place that she obviously loved dearly.

Still, by the time the children left for school, they would have had had several weeks here to recover from their long journey, he told himself, and they still had the house party and the wedding before anything would be done. There would be time enough to make a decision and he needn't wrestle with it just now. In the meantime, he could safely leave them to Miss Lytton.

For a moment he allowed himself to think of Alexandra Lytton—of dancing with her before he had known who she was, and then of dancing with her in the greengage orchard and at his own engagement ball. She was a delightful—but somewhat difficult—woman. He felt oddly at home with her, for all her prickly manner where the children were concerned.

With Pamela, though, he would have the orderly and elegant life that was necessary to his peace of mind, and even when they had children, he was certain that their children, too, would be orderly and elegant. Pamela would see to that. Or at least he hoped that she would. He longed for a family, but not one subject to the upheavals and unpredictability that he had been witness to—and an unwilling participant in—recently. He had grown up in an unhappy family and he had no desire to repeat the experience.

He strolled to the window and looked out over the orchards, now leafing out and beginning to set fruit. Nothing could calm him like the view before him. When the children were a little older, he would tell them about their inheritance and work out the details of how it would all be handled. He had been sorely tempted by Pamela's suggestion that he simply not tell them at all and keep Greengage entirely for himself, but he could not in good conscience do that. His solicitor, Alex Barry, was coming for the house party, and he would have Alex draw up the appropriate papers then so that the children would be protected should anything happen to him.

He had decided, however, that he would not mention any of this to Pamela. There was no point in distressing her now. At least, he congratulated himself, he had delayed her coming to Greengage so that Butterworth and Mrs. Melling had been able to prepare for their guests without undue interference.

Upstairs, Ned and Jennifer were once more attempting to accustom their pets to one another. Rupert no longer barked at Will or bared his teeth when brought close to the cage, but Will still retired to the far corner of his cage whenever Rupert was close. He appeared to share Browning's confidence in the ratting instincts of terriers.

"Come now, Will. Rupert won't hurt you," coaxed Ned. "Will you, Rupert?"

Rupert responded with a low, throaty growl, standing stiff-legged as he stared at Will.

"Don't let him do that, Ned! He's frightening Will!" scolded Jennifer, removing her pet's cage from harm's way.

"Well, they have to learn to get along together some-how," he replied in disgust, leaving the room with Rupert in tow. "You can't *do* that, Rupert!" he told his pet, who appeared to be listening attentively as they trotted along together.

Jennifer could hear him addressing the terrier on appropriate familial behavior as they disappeared down the passageway toward the stairs, doubtless headed for the kitchen again. She closed the door of her room firmly, then opened the door of the cage and waited while Will scampered over to her outstretched hand.

"Come along now, Will," she crooned, stroking his fur with her finger. "Rupert's gone and no one's going to hurt you."

Thus encouraged, Will was persuaded to accept one of the hazelnuts that Ned had collected from Mrs. Melling's baking supplies in the pantry. He sat on his hind legs, holding the nut in his paws as he sliced it open and daintily nibbled its meat.

When he had completed his meal, he scurried up Jennifer's sleeve to her shoulder and buried himself in her long curls. There he took his afternoon nap while Jennifer wrote in the diary that she had purchased in Shellingham. Her diary had become a great comfort to her. She had never been a confiding child, but she felt free to share her thoughts with her diary, just as her grandmother had. It was odd, she thought, that she sometimes felt closer to the grandmother she had never known than she did to those about her.

Will occasionally shifted his weight and nuzzled her ear, as though to remind her of his presence. Jennifer smiled and absentmindedly stroked him, pulling the protective curtain of hair back over him so that he slept snugly. Will was feeling much more confident after only two days at Greengage. He was both curious and affectionate. Jennifer had allowed him to explore her room freely, and he had investigated every nook and cranny with great interest. At the slightest unaccustomed sound, however, he would scamper back to the safety of his cage or her shoulder.

His other favored hiding place was the pocket of the jacket that she nearly always wore. It was a handsome little jacket of turkey red kerseymere that her mother had made for her, and Jennifer had refused to give it up when they arrived at Greengage. Alexandra had cleaned it carefully, and Jennifer still wore it almost every day, pulling it on over whatever gown she was wearing. Will apparently felt the same affection for it, and rode in its pocket with his head sticking out and his front paws clinging tightly to the pocket's rim.

Another curious thing that she was writing about in her diary was how much braver she felt because she had Will. He couldn't protect her from anything, of course. She had to protect him—it must be that, she decided, that was giving her more courage. After all, she couldn't have Will frightened or hurt. She had promised him that she would take care of him.

She had not yet confided to Clarissa that she got Will out of his cage each night and brought him to their bed. She had made a nest for him of two woolen stockings, and she placed it close to her pillow—away from Clarissa's side of the bed, of course. There Will would sleep happily until daybreak, when Jennifer would move him back to his cage. Clarissa was fond of Will, but Jennifer wasn't certain that she would like the idea of sharing their bed with him.

Suddenly the door burst open and Ned came rushing in again, Rupert hard on his heels. Will heard them and shivered, burrowing closer to Jennifer's neck. She patted him reassuringly.

"Just look at what Mrs. Melling made for us, Jenny!" he cried, bolting across the room with a metal pan covered by a checked napkin. He whipped off the napkin and proudly showed her its contents—several long slices of pastry, nicely browned and covered with cinnamon and sugar.

"She was making pies and she said that she might as well use the leftover pastry for us! Isn't she splendid? I *love* Mrs. Melling! When I am grown, I shall buy a big house and have Mrs. Melling as my cook."

"I don't want to leave Greengage," said Jennifer matter-of-factly, watching as Ned gave Rupert a bite of the pastry.

"Not ever?" demanded Ned, swallowing one of the golden-brown strips in one gulp.

She shook her head firmly. "Never. I've wanted to live here ever since I read about it in Grandmother's diary. It's a perfect place, just like she said it was. Will and I are going to stay here. Forever."

Ned looked impressed by her decisiveness. "Rupert and I are going to go exploring," he announced. "I don't think we'll go back to America first. I think we might take ship for India instead!"

"Do you think Rupert would like going on a ship?" asked Jennifer.

They both studied Rupert for a minute or two and Rupert, conscious of being the subject of the conversation, watched them carefully in return, glancing hopefully toward the pastry pan from time to time.

Alexandra, hearing them talking, had paused outside the open door and listened for a moment. Then she entered the room, smiling.

"The afternoon is beautiful—just right for a walk. Shall we go down to the pond and have a look at the ducklings?"

"May Rupert go?" asked Ned, scooping up the last piece of pastry.

"And Will?" added Jennifer, rising and reaching for her jacket and tucking Will in its pocket.

"I see no reason why they cannot." Here she turned to Ned. "But you must keep a firm grip on Rupert and try to keep him from barking."

He nodded. "Rupert's getting much better about that. I believe he understands about not scaring them."

Alexandra, looking at Rupert's bright eyes, was far less certain. Rupert might understand—she had considerable confidence in his intelligence—but she was far less certain that he agreed with the necessity of not barking.

"Keep a firm grip on him when we get to the pond," she repeated, and they all went downstairs together.

Before they could reach the bottom of the stairway, a footman hurried to the front door and opened it just as Pamela Wingate reached it and swept into the entrance hall, her mother following in her wake.

"Well, I thought that I would receive a warmer greeting than this," she observed disapprovingly to Browning, who had also just entered the hall from his library.

"I just heard the sound of carriage doors opening and closing. A thousand pardons that I was not at the door to welcome you, my dear," he said taking her arm and leading her into the room.

"Let's go back upstairs," whispered Ned, not anxious to have any more contact than necessary with Miss Wingate.

Browning heard the sound and glanced up at them. "Here is Miss Wingate, children. Miss Lytton, please bring them down so that they may greet her properly."

The small party made its way reluctantly to the foot of the steps, Ned gripping Rupert firmly and Miss Lytton smiling with determination. Miss Wingate stood watching them, a vision of elegance in her gold traveling dress and dainty swansdown muff.

"What do you have with you, Pamela?" Browning asked curiously. Following her instructions, the footman had carefully carried in a wicker basket and set it beside her.

She smiled—it was a rather unnerving, feline smile, thought Alexandra, who was watching her closely. Miss Wingate leaned down to the wicker basket and opened the lid. With a noisy cry, a pale cat with dark markings leaped out and surveyed the scene before him.

"What a pretty cat you are, Sylvester," she cooed, leaning down to pat the cat's head.

Jennifer reached up to stroke Will reassuringly, but it was too late. Will, peering from the pocket of the red jacket, had hurried up Jennifer's sleeve to the safety of her shoulder and been sighted by Sylvester. The cat sprang toward the girl with a yowl, clawing his way up the skirt of her gown. Will leaped to the floor, scampering for the nearest cover he could see—the draperies. He buried himself in the velvet folds that cascaded onto the marble floor, and Sylvester raced across the floor after him.

Rupert stood at Ned's side, quivering with indignation for as long as any self-respecting terrier could do so—and then he did what must be done. Tearing away from Ned, he flung himself after Sylvester. The cat, seeing him coming, raced up the velvet draperies, his claws leaving highly visible marks of his passing.

Pamela shrieked and Will, spurred to further efforts by the uproar, tore from behind the draperies for the closest shelter—which happened to be Richard Browning. He raced up Browning's trousers and jacket and flung himself behind one of the folds of that gentleman's cravat, as close to his neck as he could possibly manage.

Browning stood stock-still.

"Uncle! Uncle Richard! Is Will all right? Do you have him?" He looked down to see Jennifer's pleading eyes, and he reached gently for his collar and drew out the small, panting dormouse and handed it to his niece.

"I think that Will is quite all right," he said kindly. "But I believe that I would take him upstairs out of harm's way immediately."

And Jennifer did precisely that, although she stopped at the landing to look back upon the Olympian battle taking place below between Rupert and Sylvester. Sylvester appeared to think that his ability to climb must render him invulnerable, while Rupert, believing in quickness of wit and paw and teeth, had dedicated himself to bringing down the velvet drapery that provided shelter for the enemy.

In the end, despite the wails of Miss Wingate, Rupert prevailed. Browning had attempted to disengage the terrier and remove him from the scene, but his teeth were firmly planted in the velvet drape and nothing but death would have made him relinquish his prize. The drape had fallen, as had Sylvester.

Ned had watched it all, horrified, and when the drapery and the cat hit the floor together, he raced in, scooped up his pet before he could enjoy the spoils of battle, and tore back up the stairs. Rupert barked bitterly over his shoulder, promising untold horrors to Sylvester should the two of them ever meet again.

Miss Wingate, who had actually dropped her prized swansdown muff during the onslaught, attempted to pick up her cat, but Sylvester wanted no part of her. He hissed angrily and retired into the fallen drapery to regain his composure.

"Well, Richard!" she said, fairly hissing with indignation herself. "I must believe that this will make you rethink keeping those children in this house—with their animals! What *can* you have been thinking to allow them to have such pets?"

Browning was attempting to regain his own composure after the unexpected performance that he had just participated in, when he heard a most peculiar sound.

It was Miss Lytton. She was seated on the stairway, laughing. More accurately, she was weeping because of the intensity of her laughter.

"Are you all right, Miss Lytton?" he asked cautiously. He was beginning to believe that one never knew precisely what to expect. His well-ordered life was crashing about his ears.

Her shoulders shook convulsively, but she nodded. It was clear that she was trying to say something, so he waited while she regained the power to speak.

"I wanted to say that I thought Rupert acted with remarkable restraint," she managed to gasp. "Did you see how long it took before he could stand it no longer and attacked?"

Here her shoulders shook convulsively once more. "And how extraordinary it was that Jennifer's dormouse should outwit both a cat and a dog and throw himself upon your mercy, Mr. Browning."

She rose from the steps, wiped her eyes with her handerchief, and managed a brief curtsy. "I must go upstairs and see to the children," she said. "Pray excuse me."

Pamela watched her retreat with an outraged expression. "I *cannot* believe, Richard, that you allow me to be treated in such a manner! How can you let all of them go without so much as a by-your-leave? You should have raked them over the coals in no uncertain terms!"

Browning turned to her and looked at her searchingly. A most interesting question had just occurred to him.

"Pamela," he said slowly, "you told me that you have no use for animals—that you had never had a pet as a child and never wished to have one. Why in heaven's name did you choose to bring a cat with you to Greengage?"

"Are you questioning *my* actions, Richard?" she demanded. "If I choose to have a saber-toothed tiger, am I not still your fiancée, entitled to have here whatever I wish?"

"Naturally you may have whatever you wish—perhaps not a saber-toothed tiger, however," he replied, smiling slightly as he glanced down at Sylvester, who was looking disdainfully at them both. "But I do wonder why you chose to bring a cat here when you knew that there was a terrier already resident in the house."

"But not for long," she said.

When he glanced at her with a puzzled expression, she added impatiently, "Well, when they are sent away to school, you surely don't think that we will keep their pets, do you?"

For a moment Browning saw Jennifer's pleading eyes when she was asking about her dormouse and Ned's hasty rescue of his dog.

However, Pamela was quite right, of course. Who would take care of the animals when the children would be gone most of the year to school? He glanced at the wreckage of the draperies. And one certainly could not expect to have a peaceful household with cat and dog fights. Clearly, one of them would have to go.

"Naturally," he responded, and led her and her mother to the morning room to recover from the shock of their reception. "It will all be taken care of."

Pamela smiled with satisfaction and glanced back at Sylvester. As soon as the other pets were disposed of, he would also have to find another home. She had no intention of sharing Greengage with anyone.

CHAPTER 19

Fortunately for all concerned, a few house party guests arrived early, just an hour or so after the battle in the entrance hall, and the household became caught up in the new wave of activity. Alexandra breathed a sigh of relief, for that meant that her charges—and her own levity at the situation—would not come under immediate scrutiny. By the time the last guest had gone and the wedding service was over, she would be far removed from Greengage Manor. The children, though, were less fortunate. She thought they could do well enough with their uncle, but they would still have to contend with Miss Wingate and Sylvester.

Sylvester, like his mistress, quickly became a thorn in the side of virtually everyone in the household. He went slinking from floor to floor, sneaking into places where he had no business to be and where he was most certainly not welcome. Jennifer kept the door to her chamber closed at all times, but he found his way in nonetheless, and she discovered him trying to open the door to Will's cage more than once. He also prowled about in the vicinity of Ned and Rupert, seating himself on tabletops and waving a paw or a tail provocatively over the edge, just out of Rupert's reach. He also made the strategic error of going to the kitchen and allowing Mrs. Melling to discover him sitting upon the great table there, having pawed several of the fish she was preparing for dinner that evening, and leaving the skeletal remains of the best salmon.

The cook had paid an immediate visit to her master and apprised him of the problem. "There's no way to keep that cat out of the kitchen and the pantry if he's allowed to roam free," she said. "I can't answer for how much more food I shall have to throw to the pigs if he's not kept locked up."

"I will do what I can, Mrs. Melling," he promised her. "Don't worry about tossing away food, and I regret that your plans for dinner tonight have been upset."

He had a great deal of sympathy with his cook's attitude, for he was not fond of Sylvester himself. The cat had already made himself at home in the library and knocked an inkwell filled with black India ink across the papers on his desk and ruined the leather deskpad that Browning loved, leaving inky pawprints all the way across the room.

"I cannot imagine why you think it is necessary to keep Sylvester closed up in my chamber," said Pamela indignantly, when he broached the matter to her.

"I'm not suggesting that," he said mildly.

"Well, I should hope not!" She sat back a little more easily in the chair, remembering to drape herself gracefully.

"I'm suggesting that you close him up in the cage that I had Butterworth take to your chamber. I am quite certain that merely closing him in the chamber would do no good at all."

"Put Sylvester in a cage! But that's outrageous, Richard! Why don't you have that ugly little dog put into a cage?" She sat bolt upright, forgetting grace for the moment.

"Because that little dog does not create havoc in my household," he replied, his voice still calm.

"Then you have a very short memory, sir! What of your muddy drawing room and the scene in the entrance hall just this afternoon?"

"The drawing room was an accident that has not been repeated, and the scene in the drawing room would not have occurred if Sylvester had not been present."

Pamela opened her mouth to refute this, but he went on. "And neither the dog nor the dormouse has done anything to upset my staff—or to upset me. So I am afraid, Pamela, that I shall have to insist that you keep Sylvester in the cage I have provided."

"You allow yourself to be put upon by too many people—including your servants, Richard. That will not be the case after our marriage, when *our* staff will be obliged to do as I command them!"

She rose and marched stiffly from the room, her cheeks pink with anger. The only one who shared her indignation, however, was Sylvester, for even Mrs. Wingate had had an unpleasant encounter with Pamela's pet.

Nursing the ugly scratch on her arm, Mrs. Wingate had looked reproachfully at her daughter. "Why did you have to bring that nasty brute along, Pamela?" she had demanded. "You know that I dislike animals, and I had always thought you did as well."

"Well, of course I do! But I could not let those children have the upper hand, and I knew that Cousin Vincent's cat would be a match for that ugly little dog, so I borrowed him for the house party!"

Her mother looked up from dabbing iodine on her scratch. "It appeared to me that the boy's half-grown little dog has already given Sylvester a run for his money," she observed dryly. "And I understand that Sylvester has also overset the kitchen staff by eating part of tonight's dinner. It seems you were scarcely wise to bring him along, Pamela."

"I shall do just as I please!" said Pamela, leaving the chamber abruptly.

Mrs. Wingate sighed as the door slammed behind her daughter. "And so you always have, my dear—so you always have."

While Ned and Jennifer were busy protecting their pets, Clarissa was reading her way through the library's extensive contents, Michael was inspecting the gun and sword collection and haunting Gregg to learn more about hunting and guns, and Isobel was preparing herself for the arrival of Vincent Wingate. As soon as he appeared on the first afternoon of the house party, the two of them strolled arm-in-arm to the gardens.

"I heard her tell him that he would love the gardens and the orchards," Clarissa told Alexandra. "Belle doesn't seem to be herself at all. I've scarcely been able to get three coherent words from her since we came back from London."

"I wouldn't worry about it, Clarissa," Alexandra assured her. "Isobel will be herself again soon."

Privately, she was far less certain of that. She had seen the glow on the girl's face when Vincent Wingate arrived—and she knew that he had seen it, too. She had seen a speculative interest in young Wingate's eyes—but no answering glow. She knew too that a young girl like Isobel should not be spending time with Mr. Wingate without a chaperon, so she had slipped out into the garden herself, although she knew how unwelcome her appearance would be.

Keeping an eye upon Isobel as well as the children during the house party was going to be a challenge, and she was grateful that Ned was so fully occupied by protecting Rupert from the depredations of Sylvester that his own activities had slowed somewhat. They had heard that Sylvester had been placed in a cage, but they had no confidence that he would remain there. Both Ned and Jennifer stayed close to their pets.

Having considered Isobel's situation carefully, Alexandra sought out Browning on the second day of the house party to confide her fears in him. He was, after all, the girl's uncle.

"And so you think that Isobel feels an attachment for Vincent Wingate?" he asked, his winged brows rising. "Surely you cannot think that there is anything to fear in that."

Alexandra nodded. "I think there is. Hers is the attachment of a young girl for the first gentleman who has attracted her attention—but that makes it doubly powerful and doubly dangerous, depending upon the manner of man Mr. Wingate is."

He smiled at her. "You are unusually dramatic today, Miss Lytton. I had not thought you a fan of Mrs. Siddons."

Alexandra flushed at the indulgent tone of his comment. "Taking this too lightly would be a mistake, sir. She will require careful watching."

"And so you should watch her carefully," he returned casually. "That does not seem too difficult a matter."

"There are four other children," she pointed out reasonably. "And Isobel will often be with guests when I will not be. But *you* will be there, Mr. Browning, and you must not forget to take note of her—and of Mr. Wingate."

He frowned at her. "Are you suggesting that Vincent Wingate might be guilty of some impropriety?" he asked.

"I am not acquainted with the gentleman," she replied calmly, "but I do know that he consented to a stroll in the gardens—and beyond—without the benefit of a chaperon."

"Wingate may have a wild streak," he conceded, "but

he is my fiancée's cousin and he is a guest in my home. He knows what is due to his consequence and my own."

Seeing her doubtful expression, he felt himself growing irritated. He had just met with Alex Barry and made legal arrangements for the children's inheritance of Greengage and he was, for the moment, weary of hearing about them and weary of hearing someone else tell him what to do.

"You need not trouble yourself, Miss Lytton," he said in a tone of dismissal. "My niece will come to no harm under my roof."

She left the library quietly, but she was far less confident than Browning that all would be well with Isobel. She did what she could, keeping the younger children under surveillance and trying to keep a watchful eye on Isobel, too. Isobel, she knew, could see nothing save Vincent Wingate.

All too soon, however, Alexandra had a new worry to occupy her. The children had come in to admire Isobel's new gown before she went down to dinner. Ned had brought Rupert and Jennifer had Will in her pocket. They had not seen Sylvester in more than a day, but they did not believe in taking chances.

Isobel was turning in a circle for their admiration when Miss Wingate appeared in the doorway.

"Yes, you do indeed look charming, Isobel," she said pleasantly.

"Thank you, Miss Wingate," replied the girl, taken off guard by her agreeable manner. The others looked at the visitor suspiciously, but Miss Wingate continued to smile.

"That gown will be just what you need at Miss Sparrowby's," she said.

"Who is Miss Sparrowby?" asked Clarissa promptly, while the others stared at the interloper. "Is she a friend of Uncle's?"

Pamela Wingate laughed. "Scarcely that. He has never met her."

"Then why would Belle be visiting her?" demanded Clarissa.

"Because she has a very acceptable finishing school for young ladies, and that is where Isobel will be going in just a week," replied Miss Wingate.

"Uncle won't send Belle away!" Ned protested. "She likes it here at Greengage! She'd be lonely without us!"

The others simply looked at her in disbelief. Isobel had stopped smiling and slipped an arm around Jennifer.

"But you won't be here either," Miss Wingate informed him cheerfully. "You are all being sent away to school, so this will work out splendidly."

"We're all going to Miss Sparrowby's?" asked Jennifer, her voice shaking slightly.

"No, of course not. You and your other sister are too young to go there—and of course the boys will be sent elsewhere, too."

"So we'll all be going to different schools?" Jennifer's voice was breaking now.

"Except perhaps you and—and your middle sister," amended Pamela, who had yet to learn all their names. "It will be good for you to have some time apart from one another."

"But we're a *family!*" gasped Isobel, finding her voice at last. "We've managed to stay together, no matter what else has happened to us!"

"Well, it's time for a change now, my dear," replied Pamela briskly, "and you may thank your uncle for his generosity in paying for your schooling, for I assure you it will be expensive."

"Will I be able to take Rupert to school with me?" inquired Ned anxiously.

Pamela's laughter trilled through the chamber. "Hardly! Pets aren't allowed at school. But you needn't worry—we'll find a home for them somewhere."

Ned looked at her in horror, holding Rupert to him tightly, and Jennifer began to cry as Will curled down in a tight little ball in her pocket.

The hem of Alexandra's gown did not touch her heels until she reached Richard Browning's library where, not troubling to knock, she let herself in immediately.

He glanced up, surprised by the abruptness of her entrance.

"Ah, Miss Lytton," he said genially. A little relaxation with a few of his friends had done wonders for his mood, and he had decided that he had been too hard upon the governess for taking her duties to the children so seriously. He was prepared to be charitable. "I can see that you are in a particularly prickly mood and that I must take care."

That, he soon learned, was an understatement of the case.

"I fail to understand, Mr. Browning, just how a man of good sense and—I had thought—of kindly feeling would tell those children that they are being separated from one another and sent away to school and that you are giving away their pets! And you did not even trouble to do it yourself! You sent Miss Wingate to tell them!"

Browning stared at her for a long moment as he took in what she had said, and he could feel his anger rising. He could not tell whether it was anger with Miss Lytton for daring to address him in such a manner, or anger with Pamela for having done such a thing without consulting him, or anger with himself for being in this predicament at all. By the time he could find his voice, it was stiff with barely restrained rage. Pamela had been very wrong to handle things in such a manner, but he had agreed that sending the children to school was the best thing—although he was less certain about separating them and giving away their pets.

"You forget yourself, Miss Lytton. I must ask you to return to your duties and not, in the future, to concern yourself in the private matters of the family."

She stared at him in disbelief. "I would not have believed this possible," she said at last. "I had truly thought better of you, Mr. Browning, but I see that you and Miss Wingate are admirably paired. I wish you the joy that you deserve, sir—but my heart goes out to the children."

Turning, she made her way back to the children to try to cheer them as best she could. It might well be that going away to school would be the best thing in their situation, since it would put Miss Wingate at a safe distance from them.

For her own part, she was grateful that she soon would never have to see Richard Browning again. She had greatly mistaken the manner of man he was, and he had firmly reminded her of her place in the grand scheme of things. She was a servant, not someone allowed to concern herself with family affairs.

She hoped that Miss Wingate and Sylvester would give him the life he so richly deserved.

CHAPTER 20

The next two days were heartbreaking. Alexandra saw little of Richard Browning, for which she was very grateful, but every time she rounded a corner in the house she seemed to bump into Miss Wingate, who was smiling like a cat at a creampot. She could give that irritation little thought, however, for she had her hands full with the children—particularly Jennifer, who had announced that she was not going to leave Greengage Manor.

"But Uncle said that we're going to have to go to school, Jenny," Clarissa explained, for Browning himself had informed the children that Miss Wingate had been correct. "I hate it as much as you do, but we don't have a choice."

Jennifer shook her head. "I *do* have a choice. I'm not going to eat until Uncle tells me I can stay here."

"Not eat!" Ned had exclaimed in alarm. "But you'll die if you don't eat, Jenny!"

"Then I'll die at Greengage and I'll be buried in the orchard."

Clarissa, ever practical, interceded. "No one gets buried in an orchard. They bury people in the churchyard—or at the crossroads, if they can't be buried in hallowed ground."

Before Ned could pursue the meaning of this interesting comment, Jennifer shook her head. "I'll be buried in the orchard. I'm not leaving Greengage now that I've finally gotten here."

"But what about Will?" asked Ned, thinking he could divert her. "He'll die if you're not here to take care of him."

"It won't matter. If Uncle and Miss Wingate have their way, I'm not going to be here anyway and they're going to give Will away."

She turned to Alexandra, who had been listening. "Miss Lytton, will you take Will with you when you leave?"

Alexandra hesitated a moment but, when she looked into the child's anxious eyes, she gave way immediately.

"Of course. I should love to have Will." She smiled and patted Jennifer's hand.

Jennifer relaxed, but Ned, who had been trying not to think about being separated from his pet, suddenly turned upon Alexandra and threw his arms around her neck.

"And you'll take Rupert, too, won't you, Miss Lytton?" he demanded, tears running down his face. "Then I won't have to worry about whether he's all right. If he's with you, I know you'll love him and take care of him."

Governesses did not normally arrive at their posts equipped with a small menagerie, but Alexandra, looking at Ned, decided that she would worry about that when she arrived in Yorkshire.

"How could I leave Rupert?" she agreed, smiling. "After all, Will and Rupert have become companions."

That was a tremendous stretch of the present situation, which was still an armed truce at best, but it appeared to make the children feel better. The two younger ones were spending all of their time in Jennifer's room with their pets, safely locked away from Sylvester.

"I might not mind going to school," Clarissa had admitted to Alexandra privately. "I should like to learn things—but I don't want to be separated from the others.

And I don't want to live with Miss Wingate. I wish we could live here with Uncle and have you to teach us."

"Well, that is a pretty thought, Clarissa," Alexandra said comfortingly, although she could not imagine living much longer in close quarters with Richard Browning without shaking him until his teeth rattled. She could not abide selfish people, particularly those who were selfish at the expense of children. "However, since that cannot happen, it's good that you're looking forward to learning new things at school."

Michael appeared unconcerned about the matter of being sent away to school. He was once more disappearing regularly, spending most of his time away from the manor house. It was just as well that he was enjoying himself in the out of doors with Gregg, Alexandra thought, although she hoped that he was being careful with his shoulder—and that he was staying out of trouble.

And Isobel too appeared to have forgotten all about being sent away to Miss Sparrowby's. Her attention had reverted once more to Vincent Wingate, and Alexandra was doing her best to keep track of the two, but it was impossible to be with Belle every minute of the day.

It became particularly impossible when Alexandra realized that Jennifer had meant what she said. At first she had dismissed the child's announcement that she wasn't going to eat. Her food had disappeared at nuncheon and again that evening her supper tray had been polished. And so it had gone the next day.

Alexandra dined downstairs with the guests that night and was to attend the ball Browning was giving afterward for his guests and the neighbors. She had no heart for the merriment, but she knew that she needed to be present for Isobel's sake. She went upstairs after dinner to see that the other children were settled for the evening, but she stopped first in her own room to read a letter that had come in the mail that day and which a footman had given her after dinner.

She had not realized until then that she was not the only one watching Isobel with a close eye.

"Miss Lytton, may I speak with you a moment?" Michael stood in the doorway of her chamber, his hat in his hand and his eyes, for once, serious.

Alexandra looked up from her letter in surprise. Michael seldom sought her out. She had taken advantage of the moment to read the letter while Isobel was in company with the other ladies in the drawing room after dinner and the gentlemen were still at table. She knew that Vincent Wingate would be kept safely at bay by the after-dinner division of the sexes and that Clarissa was with Ned and Jennifer.

"Of course, Michael." She put away the letter and looked at him in concern. "Is there something wrong?"

He closed the door quietly behind him. "Miss Lytton, I know you've been keeping an eye on Belle, but do you know about Vincent Wingate? Do you know that he's considered a scoundrel and a cheat?"

"I know nothing about Mr. Wingate, Michael," she said slowly, "but who told you such a thing about him? Surely not one of your uncle's guests."

Michael glanced away from her, a flush rising along his cheekbones. "No. No one here told me that."

There was a long silence while Alexandra waited. She had learned that waiting was often more effective with the young than questioning. Finally Michael sighed and sat down.

"I've been borrowing a horse from the stable and riding over to the Blue Angel," he admitted.

When she still didn't speak, he went on. "It's an inn a mile or two from here. I heard about it when we were at the fair, and I've gone there a few times when I've gotten bored."

"To gamble?" she asked.

He nodded slowly. "And I've won," he said, grinning suddenly. "I told Belle that I had no need of a marked deck." His grin faded. "We may need the money if we have to leave Greengage."

"You don't mean that you're thinking about running away again?" Alexandra's heart sank. She hadn't considered that possibility—not after the horrible experience they had had on their journey here. Even being sent away to school seemed a better choice—but perhaps not to the children.

Michael continued grimly. "I've heard a lot of gossip at the inn, some of it about our uncle and his guests. That's where I heard them talking about Wingate. The Angel is a posting inn, and people stop there on their way to London. One of the guests waiting for a change of teams said Wingate had been caught cheating at a club in London, and that now he can't gamble anywhere there because no one will trust him."

Alexandra shook her head. "We don't know that's true, Michael—not just because of a stranger's gossip at an inn."

"I know," he admitted, "but it's enough to make me wish he weren't trying to cozy up to Belle."

Alexandra could not argue with him about that. "Surely your uncle would know if such a thing had occurred."

Michael shrugged. "Perhaps—but he's Miss Wingate's cousin, you know. Perhaps he wouldn't believe the story. But there's another thing," he said, more grimly still. "Many of the people that go to the taproom of the inn have lived here all their lives—long before Uncle came to Greengage. They knew our grandmother and our great-grandparents, too."

Alexandra waited, knowing that there was more coming.

"When I was there this afternoon, one of them said that he had heard that our great-grandmother had willed Greengage Manor to her twin grandchildren."

Alexandra stared at him. Whatever she had expected, it had not been this.

"Do you see what this means, Miss Lytton?" he asked finally. "Greengage Manor was left to our uncle—and to our mother. Why has he said nothing to us about that?"

Alexandra's mind was whirling. She had not always thought well of Richard Browning and his behavior toward the children, but she had never suspected him of such dishonorable conduct as this.

"I wished to speak to him as soon as I got back, but of course he is with guests."

"We will speak to him together, Michael. Tomorrow morning. There will be too many people with him the rest of the day."

He nodded grimly. "I most certainly want to speak with him."

"Don't upset the others with this just yet," she cautioned him. "There will be time enough to talk about this later, and they have enough to distress them."

There was a knock at the door and Ned appeared. "Miss Lytton?" he said in a whisper. "I'm scared. Jenny hasn't eaten in two days, and now she just fell over in a heap onto the floor. Clarissa told me to come and get you."

Alexandra rose, dropping the letter to the floor. "What do you mean, she hasn't eaten? All of the food has been gone from her plate."

Ned dropped his eyes. "She told me to give it to Rupert, so I did. But I thought she'd give up and eat."

The three of them ran down the passage to Jennifer's

room, where Clarissa was standing by the bed, trying to get her sister's attention.

"I picked her up and put her on the bed, but she won't talk to me, Miss Lytton! Do you think she's dying, just as she said she would?" Clarissa, usually calm and straightforward, was weeping.

"Nonsense! Of course she isn't dying!" said Alexandra reassuringly. She rang the bell for the maid. "We'll order some gruel and I shall see to it that she eats it."

That, however, proved easier to say than to do. By the time the gruel had arrived Jennifer had opened her eyes, but she wouldn't open her mouth to take a bite of it.

"Please, Jenny!" begged Clarissa. "You're going to get awfully sick if you don't eat. You've already fainted."

Alexandra, looking at the frail little figure on the bed, felt her heart twist. Jennifer had already been as thin as a child could possibly be. The slight bit of weight she had acquired since arriving at Greengage seemed to have disappeared overnight, and she railed at herself for not noticing it immediately.

Isobel appeared in the doorway, with Michael just behind her, and ran to her sister's side.

"Jenny, are you all right?" she asked, bending over the little girl. "Michael came and told me that you'd fainted."

Jenny smiled when Isobel patted her cheek and smoothed back her hair. "You'll eat something now, won't you?" Isobel begged.

The smile faded from Jenny's face and she shook her head. "No. I'm not going to eat unless I can stay here, Belle."

Isobel looked at Alexandra with terrified eyes. "She means it, Miss Lytton! What are we going to do?"

"We will see to it that she eats something," said Alexandra firmly, although she was very far from being convinced that they would be able to manage it.

Ned appeared at the bedside with Will's nest of woolen socks and tucked him in next to Jennifer, who looked fondly at her pet and rubbed his head with her finger.

"You'll be happy with Miss Lytton, Will. She'll take good care of you," she whispered to the dormouse, a tear running down her cheek and onto his fur.

When Alexandra looked up next, she realized that Isobel and Michael were no longer in the room. For a moment she considered going back downstairs to the ball so that Isobel would have a chaperon but, after looking once more at Jennifer's small pinched face, she decided that she must stay. One evening could not make that great a difference to Belle but it might very well make a difference to Jennifer. So she settled herself next to the bed with Ned, Clarissa, and Rupert, and they spent the evening talking to Jennifer and trying to tempt her with everything from Will's hazelnuts to plum cake, for Ned made a special journey to the kitchen to ask Mrs. Melling's assistance.

Mrs. Melling herself made the journey upstairs, bearing a tray of delicacies from the supper that would be served later that evening. However, not even the jellies or syllabub or even the lemon ice was enough to persuade Jennifer to eat, and the cook went away shaking her head.

It seemed to Alexandra that she had never endured a longer evening. She could not think of a single thing to say to Jennifer that would make her believe that everything would be all right and that she should therefore eat. She was losing everything that was most important to her—the closeness and support of her brothers and sisters, Greengage Manor, and Will.

It had occurred to her that if Michael's information about their great-grandmother's will were accurate, something might be done about the children's situation.

However, even if it happened to be true, their future undoubtedly would still lie in the hands of the uncle. At the
moment she could see no way out of the dilemma, but
she had every intention of taking up the matter with
Richard Browning the next morning.

Finally all three of the children fell asleep, and
Alexandra left Ned and Rupert in bed with the girls, all
of them tucked under the covers—but with Ned and Jennifer safely between Rupert and Will. She closed the
door quietly to be certain that Sylvester could not join
them if he were prowling about, and went to Michael's
room. There was no sign of him, although clothing had
been tossed carelessly about the chamber.

Sighing, she made herself presentable and went downstairs to the ball. Supper had been served, and
Alexandra glanced through the rooms, looking for Isobel. She could find no sign of her, however, and after a
few minutes she began to grow alarmed.

In the morning room, which had been set with card
tables, she saw Mrs. Pendergrass, whom she had met a
week ago when that lady had come to Greengage Manor
for the express purpose of meeting "dear Deidre's great-
grandchildren." She had shown a marked interest in
each of the children and had learned their names—and
the names of their pets—before departing.

At the moment Mrs. Pendergrass was enjoying a glass
of champagne, but she looked up and smiled as Alexandra approached.

"Good evening, Miss Lytton," she said pleasantly.
"How are Clarissa and Jennifer and Ned? I've had the
pleasure of seeing Isobel and Michael already this
evening."

"Michael?" said Alexandra in surprise. "Has he been
to the ball?"

Mrs. Pendergrass nodded. "He was not dancing, of

course, but he was very well dressed. Deidre would have been very proud of his appearance and his manners."

"But what was he doing if he wasn't dancing? Was he playing cards?"

Mrs. Pendergrass chuckled. "Neither. He told me that since you had been called upstairs, he had appointed himself Isobel's chaperon."

"Indeed? Actually, ma'am, it is Isobel that I was going to ask you about. Have you seen her?"

"Not since some time before supper. I'm not certain just how long ago it might have been. I stopped watching the dancers and came in here to play whist."

"And you haven't seen Michael since then, either?"

Mrs. Pendergrass shook her head. "And I'm sorry that I did not. He reminds me in some ways of his uncle at that age."

"Indeed?" repeated Alexandra automatically, her mind working furiously. Normally she would have been interested in hearing Mrs. Pendergrass enlarge upon that subject, but not at this particular moment.

"Richard was a handsome boy when he came here, but you never saw an unhappier lad. It took Deidre more than a year to get him to smile. Now, young Michael has a ready laugh and a merry heart—but they cover a good deal of unhappiness, too."

"Yes, I know that you are right, ma'am," agreed Alexandra, looking at the old lady's shrewd eyes. "I'm afraid that all of them are unhappy."

"Perhaps it's time for Richard to remember how long it took his grandmother to make him feel safe here. I think he's forgotten."

Alexandra smiled at her and patted her hand. "And I know that you are correct about that, as well, ma'am. I should like very much for you to speak with Mr. Browning about that—but if you'll forgive me, I must go and find the children now."

She made one more thorough circuit of the ballroom and the connecting rooms that had been opened for the evening. The doors were open to the warm spring air, and she walked the length of the terrace, trying to peer out into the gardens and to listen for familiar voices. She did not see Isobel or Michael—or Vincent Wingate. She did catch a glimpse of Richard Browning, but he was engaged with several of his guests, and she decided not to approach him.

Instead, she hurried back upstairs to see if Isobel might have gone to her chamber. If she had needed to make some small repair or to straighten her hair, she might have come back there. Or she might have come up once more to check on Jennifer. Since she had not seen Michael or Mr. Wingate either, however, she did not believe in her heart what she was telling herself.

In Jennifer's room, everyone was still sleeping quietly. Michael's room was still undisturbed. When she entered Isobel's chamber, the first thing she saw was a folded slip of paper on her pillow.

She unfolded it quickly and read it, her heart sinking.

The note was to her from Isobel. She had eloped with Vincent Wingate. She would, she wrote, send for the children as soon as they were settled.

CHAPTER 21

"She is *exactly* like her mother! Running away without a thought for how her actions will affect anyone else!"

Richard Browning was furious, small white creases showing around his mouth as he tried to restrain his anger from erupting, and Alexandra was grateful that she had waited until they reached the library to tell him about Isobel's note. It was unfortunate that Miss Wingate had insisted upon coming, too, but it had been unavoidable.

"Behaving in the most senseless manner possible!" he continued, bringing down his fist on the library table and causing a vase of flowers to vibrate dangerously.

"She certainly had no consideration for *my* family!" agreed Pamela Wingate, who was fully as outraged as Browning. "Why, what will people think if they hear that Vincent ran away with—with a *gypsy* child!"

Browning turned to glare at his fiancée, but she was not to be intimidated. "Well, you must admit, Richard, that one would *not* wish it known that one's cousin married a girl with a background such as hers. Even though she is your niece, she has not had your advantages."

Browning laughed briefly. "On the contrary, she has had some of the very same advantages."

"Well, I certainly don't know what you're talking about, Richard, but I do know that Vincent has been very much put upon!"

"*Vincent* has been put upon?" he asked incredulously. "Do you mean to say that he has been kidnapped by a sixteen-year-old girl?"

"Well, you certainly cannot imagine that he would have thought of this *himself!*" she protested. "After all, Vincent is a handsome, eligible man. He could have his pick of young women."

"From what I have just heard from Freddie Taverner, Vincent is no longer quite so eligible as you would suggest, Pamela. My niece may be thoughtless, but she is young and very impressionable. He has no business taking advantage of her."

Before Miss Wingate could express her outrage at his comment, he turned once more to Alexandra. "Miss Lytton, I don't suppose she mentions just what their destination is."

Alexandra nodded. "They are on their way to Paris."

"Well, at least she has told me more than her mother did. I have some hope of catching up to them before they take ship."

He turned to ring the bell for Butterworth, and when he did, he glanced at the wall beside the bell pull. A pair of dueling pistols normally hung next to the pull, but tonight one of them was missing.

"Splendid!" he exclaimed, yanking on the cord. "I daresay one of my guests has borrowed a pistol for a duel at dawn—probably to take place on my terrace!"

Alexandra stared at him, her heart suddenly in her throat.

"What's wrong now, Miss Lytton?" he demanded. "You looked cool enough when you were telling me about Isobel eloping with Vincent Wingate. Why would a missing pistol distress you?"

She could scarcely bring herself to say what had just crossed her mind. "It is Michael," she said in a low voice.

"I can't find Michael either, and Mrs. Pendergrass said that he had appointed himself Isobel's chaperon. He may have gone after them."

Browning stared at her for a moment, then strode toward the library door just as Butterworth entered.

"You rang, sir?" he said, bowing.

"Have my horse saddled immediately!" he said briefly. "And tell Barrett I will be changing to riding dress!"

Butterworth bowed once more and hurried from the room. A sense of urgency hung thickly in the air now.

"You don't think that the boy took a gun to shoot Vincent, do you?" exclaimed Miss Wingate, who had just put it all together. She wheeled upon Alexandra. "If you had done your duty and taken care of these terrible children, none of this would be happening!"

Alexandra said nothing because she was of the same mind as Miss Wingate. The children's world seemed to be crumbling around them and she had not been able prevent any of it.

"That is quite enough, Pamela! Miss Lytton tried to warn me about Isobel and your cousin, but I paid no attention to her. The fault is mine."

He walked from the room, ignoring Pamela's protests, and was just starting up the stairs when Alistair Trumbull and his wife, two of his guests, came hurrying toward him.

"Richard!" cried Mrs. Trumbull. "Wait a moment! We must speak with you!"

Reluctantly he turned back toward them. "Is there something wrong, Diana?" he asked impatiently.

"I should say so!" she exclaimed, holding up an empty velvet box. "My emeralds are gone!"

He looked at her blankly for a moment, then turned and came back down the stairs. "What are you saying, Diana?"

"I'm saying that they were stolen, Richard! We went

back to our chamber because we were going to retire early, and my trunk was open and my jewels gone! Thank heavens I was wearing my mother's diamonds tonight so that at least I still have them!"

A murmur of alarm swept through the guests, who had gathered at the sound of raised voices, and the hall was soon flooded by people rushing back to their rooms to see if anything had been stolen from them.

"We will look into the matter directly, Diana," he assured her and hurried up to his room to change.

By the time Browning had donned his riding clothes and returned to the entrance hall, it was crowded with guests who had discovered that they too had been robbed. Alexandra felt considerable pity for the man as he listened to the guests calling out to him what they had lost. His dark face lost some of its life and color, but his eyes remained bright and determined.

"I will be back in a short time," he told the gathered group. "In the meantime, I would like for you to remain downstairs while my butler has the servants conduct a search of the rooms. If the missing items have been left anywhere within the manor house, they will find them."

Here he turned to his solicitor. "Alex, I leave you in charge. Butterworth, you will conduct the search and report directly to Mr. Barry."

"But, Richard, where are you going?" asked his friend.

"I have a family matter to attend to first," he answered briefly. "I will be back as quickly as I can."

"Richard, Butterworth should be reporting to *me!* I should be the one left in charge!" complained Pamela, but her protests fell on the empty air, for her quarry had already left.

Alexandra was waiting outside where the groom had Browning's horse, saddled and ready. She had hoped to have the opportunity to say something about Jennifer, but she could see that she would have no chance. Browning swung quickly into the saddle, but before he touched his spurs to his mount, he turned and looked down at her.

"You do realize, Miss Lytton, that this means that Michael may not have taken the gun to go after young Wingate. He may very well have taken it as protection for this robbery. I told Butterworth to search the boy's room first."

Horrified by his words, Alexandra shrank back. He could not possibly believe such a thing. For a moment she remembered what Michael had said about gambling, but she had not believed that showed any genuine weakness of character—particularly when it seemed he was doing it to help his brother and sisters. She had hoped that she would have the opportunity to talk with Browning about his nephew soon, just as she hoped to talk to him about several pressing issues.

When she went back inside, she went directly to Michael's room and stood in the doorway while Butterworth and one of the footmen looked through Michael's things. After a few minutes, the old butler turned to her and shook his head.

"There is nothing here, Miss Lytton," he assured her.

"Thank heavens!" She leaned gratefully against the door. She had not believed that there would be, but in the face of Browning's accusation and her own knowledge of Michael's other activities, she had suddenly been afraid.

When they were about to enter Pamela Wingate's room, that lady came rushing down the passage, protesting volubly.

"You will *not* enter my room or my mother's! I will not allow such wanton disregard for our dignity!" she told them.

"But, Miss Wingate," said Butterworth, attempting to explain, "the master said that we were even to search his own chambers."

"That is up to him!" she replied, standing in front of her door. "But you will *not* search *my* chamber!" And she walked inside and slammed the door.

Alexandra waited until they had searched Isobel's room and her own, then walked to the chamber where the rest of the children lay sleeping and opened the door quietly for the two men to enter.

"That will not be necessary, Miss Lytton," Butterworth assured her, and they moved to another passage to continue their search.

Unwilling to return to her own room and feeling in need of comfort, Alexandra went into the children's room and drew a chair close to their bed. If there had been space enough, she would have tucked herself in among them.

As there was not, she simply sat next to them and waited for the dawn to break. There were not many hours left in the night. For once in her life, however, she wished that the night would linger. She was fearful of what daybreak would reveal.

CHAPTER 22

Mrs. Melling, Butterworth, and the rest of the servants had had a long and sleepless night. They had served refreshments to the disgruntled guests until they were allowed to return to their chambers, and by that time the staff had to begin preparations for the morning. Fires had to be lit, coal scuttles filled, hot water taken upstairs, breakfast cooked.

Therefore, Mrs. Melling was not best pleased to see Sylvester perched on her table, placing his paw neatly on the dough she had just rolled out for apple tarts. She sent him packing from the kitchen, but even if her master had been home to complain to, she would not have done it.

As she told the scullery maid, "Betty, that poor man could not bear to hear another trouble more than those he's heard during the past few hours."

She glanced toward the ceiling. "And as for the poor lamb upstairs who isn't eating, I daresay he hasn't even heard about that yet. And heaven knows that Miss Wingate will offer him no support. Leaning on her will be like leaning on a broken stick."

The two women sniffed simultaneously to express their opinion of Miss Wingate, Mrs. Melling disposed of the pastry and began her work again, and Betty chopped apples for the tarts.

Despite her fears, or perhaps because of them, Alexandra had arisen early, before any light at all was visible. She wandered downstairs, knowing that all would be still except for the servants going quietly about their business. She let herself out the door and stood watching the drive. For once she did not think of going down to the orchard, even when the first rays of light brightened the gardens and the tops of the trees.

Instead, she stood and waited. Surely they would return soon. She could not accept the possibility that Browning might not find them, or that something might have happened to one—or more—of them.

Butterworth had told her gravely that they had found no sign of any of the lost jewelry, although Alex Barry had recorded a lengthy list of missing items.

"The thief would need to have had a pair of saddlebags at least, miss," he had told her, and he shook his head sadly. "It's no better than highway robbery—only it happened right here under our own roof."

Finally she decided that she would at least go in for a cup of coffee, and she let herself back in to the entrance hall. As she did so, she saw Sylvester slipping into the drawing room.

Wonderful, she thought. Now that he was out of his cage, they would have Sylvester to contend with once more. Instead of having her coffee first, she climbed the stairs swiftly to be certain that the door to the children's room was closed so that there would be no immediate excitement for Rupert and Will.

Satisfied that all was well there—or as well as it could be until she could persuade Jennifer to eat—she went back downstairs, trying to think of something she could do that would be helpful. Failing in that, she drank two cups of coffee and paced back and forth, waiting for any sound of movement from the drive.

Finally she heard the crunch of gravel, and rushed to the door in time to see Michael dismount and then turn to help his sister from the curricle driven by Richard Browning. Isobel's face was tearstained, but there was no other sign of emotion. All three of them filed silently into the hall, and Browning gestured toward the library.

"You need to come in, too, Miss Lytton," he said tonelessly and closed the door behind them.

He poured himself a glass of brandy and sat down wearily. Alexandra too sat down at his gesture, but Isobel and Michael remained standing close to one another.

"You were quite correct about the pistol, Miss Lytton," he told her, sipping his brandy and staring at the children. "Michael had taken it, and apparently had every intention of using it."

"If necessary," said Michael flatly, with no hint of his usual deviltry. "But it wasn't."

"But where is Vincent Wingate?" asked Alexandra. "What happened?"

"He left me," said Isobel. "When Michael caught up with us, he told Vincent that he would shoot him if he tried to take me with him. Vincent just laughed and said that I wasn't that important."

She stared down at the toes of her slippers for a moment. "I thought that Vincent cared for me and intended to marry me, but that's not what he said when Michael arrived. He said that he was just taking me along for amusement."

Alexandra knew how much it had cost Isobel to make such an admission, and her heart went out to the girl. Browning, however, felt no such compassion.

"I have waited until we were here, under my own roof, so that you could explain to me just why you did something so senseless as running away with the first young fribble who makes eyes at you." His tone was abrupt, and he looked at her pitilessly. "I am waiting for your explanation."

Isobel threw up her chin. "I thought that Vincent would marry me and that I would be able to offer a home to my brothers and sisters. We have none now."

"That is true, Mr. Browning," said Alexandra. "She wrote in her note that she would send for the children as soon as they were settled in Paris."

A long silence fell over the library while Browning stared at Isobel and the two others watched him. Whatever he had expected her to answer, it had not been this.

"You have a home here," he began, but she did not allow him to finish.

"We do *not* have a home here! You are separating us from one another and sending us away! That is not a home! If I had married Vincent, we could have had a real home and all of us could have lived together!"

Michael cleared his throat. "As to the matter of a home, Uncle," he said, "I have heard gossip that our great-grandmother left Greengage Manor to her twin grandchildren. Is there any truth in that?"

Once again quiet fell over the library, and once again all three of them watched him carefully. Finally, his gaze still directed at Michael, he nodded.

"It is true. Half of Greengage Manor was left to your mother, and therefore half of it is yours."

"Then why didn't you tell us?" Michael demanded. "Because you plan to keep it all for yourself?"

Browning stood up abruptly and walked to the window, his back to them. "No! Although I would love to do so, I admit it."

"And I would imagine that's exactly what you planned to do!" Michael clearly thought he had caught his uncle in a lie. "You were going to send us all away, and keep Greengage for yourself!"

Browning shook his head. "I had my solicitor, Alex Barry, draw up the papers after he arrived here for the house party. Should anything happen to me, you will all be provided for and Greengage will be entirely yours. As it is, half of the property belongs to the five of you."

"Then why didn't you *tell* us that, Uncle?" asked Isobel. "And why are you sending us all away as though we don't belong here? I wouldn't have run away with Vincent if I had thought that we had a home."

For the first time since she had met him, Alexandra saw Browning's shoulders suddenly slump. He no longer appeared to be the eagle, descending upon its prey—or the perfect gentleman, in control of every emotion.

"I see now that I should have told you sooner," he admitted, turning back toward the brother and sister. "However, as for the schools, I still believe that it is best that all of you be sent to receive an education."

"Mrs. Pendergrass mentioned to me that your grandmother had to spend quite some time with you before you felt secure here at Greengage," said Alexandra, suddenly entering the fray. "Are you saying, Mr. Browning, that when you first came here your grandmother immediately sent *you* away to school?"

Browning looked into her eyes for a long moment, and finally he shook his head. "No. You are quite right to remind me, Miss Lytton. My grandmother did *not* send me away immediately. In fact, I stayed here for two years—with a tutor—before attending Cambridge. And she told me then that I did not need to go if I did not wish to do so."

"Then perhaps that would be the best way to handle your nieces and nephews," suggested Alexandra. "Since you think so highly of your grandmother and the way that she treated you, following her example might well be the most satisfactory choice for everyone concerned."

For the first time in what seemed like days, Browning allowed himself to smile. "I believe, Miss Lytton, that you have pointed out a home truth to me. I can do no better than to follow my grandmother's example."

"Do you mean it, Uncle—that we may all stay here at Greengage?" demanded Isobel.

Richard Browning nodded, the faintest trace of a smile creasing his lips. "I believe that your great-grandmother would approve of that."

Michael's face brightened with one of his lightning smiles as Isobel hugged him.

"May we go up and tell the others that we are staying, Uncle?" she begged.

He nodded once again, his smile deepening as he watched them.

They turned to race from the library, but at the door Isobel stopped and ran back to hug Browning and kiss him on the cheek. "Thank you, Uncle!" she cried, and then the pair ran to the stairs and Alexandra could hear them clattering toward the third floor.

Suddenly she remembered Sylvester and pictured the door to the children's room flying open with the pets tucked in bed and Sylvester lurking just outside. Alexandra rose and went racing up the stairs after Isobel and Michael.

Browning watched her in astonishment. "Miss Lytton!" he called. "Wait! We have other matters to discuss."

She was gone, however, and he thoughtfully finished his brandy and then started up the stairs at a more sedate pace.

As Alexandra had feared, Sylvester had been awaiting his opportunity, and when Isobel and Michael opened the door to the children's room, he shot in with them. He raced toward Will's cage, but saw to his disgust that it was empty. A quick survey of the room revealed a slight twitching at the edge of the bed and he caught sight and scent of the dormouse at the same time that Will sighted Sylvester.

Will shot deep under the covers, and Sylvester leaped high into the air, landing squarely—and misguidedly—on Ned, who sat up abruptly and yelled. To say that pandemonium broke loose would not have been to overstate the case. Rupert awoke to the nightmare vision of a cat on his bed and threw himself at Sylvester, sharp terrier teeth flashing. A yowl that would have awakened the dead tore through the air as Rupert made contact with the cat's flank, and Clarissa shrieked when Sylvester ran across her, claws flying.

In the battle among the tangled covers, Will decided that safety for a small dormouse lay elsewhere, and he leaped from the bed to the floor, aiming for the safety of the area under a nearby desk. Sylvester sighted him, however, and followed in hot pursuit. Jennifer, who had awakened groggily, saw what was happening and tried to jump from the bed. She wasn't strong enough, however, and merely managed a tumble onto the floor.

"Will!" she called weakly.

Whether Will recognized his name or not remained a matter of discussion for some time to come, but everyone agreed that the dormouse suddenly veered from his course to the desk and doubled back, straight under the flying body of Sylvester, and Jennifer snatched him up, holding him as high as she could manage.

Sylvester regained his balance, turned, and leaped for Will, raking his claws down Jennifer's thin arms and yowling madly. Michael scooped Jennifer and Will up from the floor and Rupert flung himself upon Sylvester once more.

Sylvester managed to break away and make a run for

the door, and Clarissa threw a pillow at his retreating form.

A crowd had arrived at the door in time to see the last scene of the battle. Alexandra, Browning, and Miss Wingate, who had been awakened by the racket, all witnessed it.

"Richard!" Miss Wingate screamed. "They are attacking my cat!"

"I believe, Pamela, that you have gotten that reversed. Sylvester appears to have been the perpetrator."

Suddenly he caught sight of the blood on Jennifer's arms, and his casual attitude disappeared. Striding over to her, he turned back the sleeves of her gown so that he could see the long gouges.

"I will take care of her, Mr. Browning," said Alexandra, hurrying to her room for the things she needed to cleanse and medicate the scratches.

As he placed the child on the bed, Browning could see how thin and pale she had become.

"What's wrong with her?" he asked abruptly, looking at her brothers and sisters.

"She hasn't been eating, Uncle," said Ned. "She said that she wasn't going to eat anything until you told us that we could stay here."

Browning's face flushed. This was all it lacked, he thought, to show him the error of his ways.

"If that is the case, I think we should send Nan down to Mrs. Melling for the largest breakfast that she can prepare," he informed them, nodding toward the little maid who had appeared in the doorway.

Jennifer's eyes flew open. "Do you mean it, Uncle?" she asked, holding Will close to her. "Are we staying at Greengage?"

He nodded and stroked her thin cheek. "For as long as you wish," he said. "This is your home."

"Forever?" she asked, determined to have it stated clearly.

"Forever," he assured her.

A shout went up from the children, and when it had faded away, Miss Wingate's outraged voice could be heard.

"Richard, have you lost your senses?" she demanded. "We agreed that these children are to go to school!"

"I believe, Pamela, that I have just now found my senses," he informed her. "I meant exactly what I said. This is their home and they will stay here for as long as they please to do so."

Her dainty face was scarlet now. "Then you cannot expect *me* to live here, Richard! Nor, if you treat me in such a manner, can you expect me to marry you!"

He nodded. "I believe that you are correct, Pamela. I think that it would not be fair of me to expect you to marry me under these circumstances. When we became engaged, I had no family—but now I have five children. Expecting you to care for them is not fair to you, and I agree that you should have your freedom."

Miss Wingate, who had not expected him to give her up so easily, stared at him in disbelief, then turned and flounced from the room.

The younger children started to raise a cheer, but Alexandra shook her head and motioned to them to be quiet, so they satisfied themselves with bouncing on the bed, to the consternation of Will, who disliked the upheaval, and to the joy of Rupert, who loved it.

The happiness of the moment quickly abated, however, for Butterworth appeared, his expression grim.

"Your guests are waiting downstairs to speak with you, sir," he told Browning.

For a moment Browning had forgotten the robbery, but now he knew he would be obliged to confront that problem. His guests had all been robbed in his home, and he had no idea who was responsible. Alexandra watched him leave, feeling more pity for him than she had last night. For a man accustomed to being in complete control, matters had gone badly awry.

"What's wrong with Uncle?" Clarissa asked. "He was so happy with us, but then he became grim so suddenly."

Alexandra explained to them what had happened the night before, and Ned looked at her, his eyes wide.

"Do you mean there were real robbers here in our house?"

Alexandra nodded. "At least one," she agreed.

"But how did he get in?" asked Michael, frowning as he thought it over.

"Butterworth said that they didn't find any sign that someone had broken in, and the only open window was on the third floor," said Alexandra.

"Then it had to be someone inside the house," said Michael. "And it had to be done while everyone was downstairs at dinner and the ball."

"That still leaves a good many people," observed Alexandra, "both guests and servants."

"But most of Uncle's servants have been with him forever," objected Clarissa. "I wouldn't think that any of them would be party to a robbery."

Isobel had been sitting quietly, her face flushed. "Vincent left the dining room while the gentlemen were drinking after dinner. I know because Michael came to get me and tell me that Jennifer was ill. As we came up the stairs, I saw him in the entrance hall below us."

"Well, it's true that no one would pay any attention to him if he went to that wing of the house, because his own chamber was there," Alexandra agreed slowly, watching Nan place a heavy breakfast tray on the bed. Jennifer began with porridge and tea, while Ned attacked the toast and eggs, giving Rupert a slice of toast and Will a strawberry.

"But if that's true," she continued, "then the jewels have gone with him. He can easily sell them in Paris."

"I don't think he's going directly to Paris," said Isobel. "At least not directly. He said that we would spend a little time at the seaside before we sailed because he was waiting for someone."

"So he had a partner," mused Michael, who had already acted as judge and jury for Wingate. He was certain of the man's guilt.

"Did the thief take very many jewels?" asked Clarissa.

Alexandra nodded. "Butterworth said that he would have needed at least a pair of saddlebags."

"Then Vincent didn't have them with him," said Isobel, her expression brightening a little. Even though Vincent Wingate had not turned out to be the man she thought him, she would prefer that he not be a thief. "He wasn't carrying anything at all."

"If Wingate took the jewels, then he must have stashed them somewhere close so that his partner could pick them up and bring them to him."

Michael looked at them, his eyes brightening. "It would have to be someplace close at hand, because he didn't have time to go far before he left with you, Belle. And I was watching you both during most of the ball."

"Did he go outside at all?" asked Clarissa suddenly. "The doors to the terrace were open, weren't they?"

Alexandra, Michael, and Isobel all nodded, their minds churning busily.

"Well, there's the garden," said Clarissa.

Michael shook his head. "His partner would have to come too close to the house. It has to be something a little farther."

"The greengage orchard," murmured Jennifer, who

had been listening drowsily. She had leaned back on her pillow after eating her porridge. "That's far enough away, isn't it?"

"Let's go!" said Michael. "It's scarcely more than daybreak, so his partner might not have come yet."

He and Isobel and Alexandra were the only ones dressed, and they went hurrying down the stairs, with Michael, fleet of foot, flying on ahead of them.

"It's not fair!" wailed Clarissa. "Wait for me to get dressed!"

She and Ned scrambled for their clothes, aided by the nips of Rupert. Only Jennifer and Will remained in bed, although Will was watching alertly from his nest.

"I'm closing the door, Jenny!" Clarissa cried on her way out. "Sylvester won't be able to get in, and I'll send Nan to stay with you!"

Browning and his unhappy guests were in the drawing room when he saw Michael, trailed by Alexandra and Isobel, go running across the dew-soaked meadow to the greengage orchard. They were inordinately eager to get there, he thought absently, wondering what on earth they could be doing. A few minutes later he was startled to see Ned, Clarissa, and Rupert trot smartly by in the pony cart, traveling the lane that led around between the orchards.

"If you will excuse me," he murmured to his guests, "I will be back in just a few minutes. I appear to have pressing business in the greengage orchard."

The guests, who had been trying to decide whether to send for the Bow Street Runners, stared at one another.

"Browning is growing more peculiar with each passing day," observed Alistair Trumbull. "What pressing business could he possibly have in the orchard?"

A few of them shook their heads as they saw him running across the meadow. The consensus of opinion was that the poor fellow was giving way under the duress of the robbery.

"Look!" called Isobel in excitement as they ran down the green alley between the trees. "There's something down there near where we picnicked last!"

Unfortunately, the something proved to be an abandoned basket, forgotten after that last outing. The three of them looked around hopefully, but they could see nothing else unusual, and they were standing there forlornly when Browning arrived. All of them looked bedraggled, their clothing and shoes soaked by the dew.

"Whatever sent you all flying down here?" he demanded. "What is the emergency?"

"We thought that we had figured out where the jewels might have been left," said Michael, proceeding to explain their line of thought to his uncle.

They walked slowly back to the manor house, discussing the possibilities, as the guests watched them from the windows. No one paid any particular attention to a messenger arriving with a note for Miss Wingate.

Upstairs, Jennifer and Will were resting while the little maid cleared up the remains of breakfast. Seeing that both her charges appeared to be asleep, she decided to carry the tray down to the kitchen. She got no more than two steps down the passage before being stopped by Miss Wingate, however, who informed her that she needed a footman to carry her baggage downstairs.

The subsequent noise in the passageway aroused Jennifer. Curious about what was taking place, she opened the door a tiny crack and peered out at the trunks and boxes that the footman was stacking outside Miss Wingate's chamber.

"Well, I *do* think that you are wise to call off the engagement, Pamela," Mrs. Wingate was saying. "I do not think that you could *possibly* be expected to look after children who would actually sell their mother's jewelry! Heaven only knows what they would do next! Why, they might even have taken *your* jewelry to sell!"

Mrs. Wingate paused in what she was saying to look at her daughter in horror. "Why, do you suppose that *they* are responsible for the robbery last night?" she demanded.

Pamela shrugged. "I would put nothing past them," she replied. "And Richard had the boy's chamber searched first last night, so he must have thought the same thing."

She stomped one tiny foot on the floor. "I cannot believe that Richard Browning would *dare* to criticize Vincent's behavior when those children are so clearly ruffians!"

Jennifer felt Will suddenly began to shake and tuck himself more tightly against her neck. She glanced at the mound of baggage and saw a pair of dark eyes glaring at them—fortunately, however, glaring from inside his cage.

She patted Will and whispered to him reassuringly.

"And Vincent is quite the kindest of men, Mother," Pamela continued. "Do you know that he sent me a note telling me that he will collect Sylvester from me? He's going to Paris, and yet he wants to be certain of taking his cat along, too."

Mrs. Wingate sniffed. She was less impressed by her nephew's dedication to Sylvester. "All I can say is that it's a good thing that cat is traveling in his cage instead of his basket. At least he can't escape from the cage."

"Vincent particularly asked me to have Sylvester travel in this cage so that he would have more room," Pamela informed her. "He is going to use the travel basket for Sylvester's supplies. He is the most considerate man I know!"

Jennifer closed the door gently and hurried over to the wardrobe. "We have to get dressed, Will," she whispered.

It took her considerably longer than usual to dress and to comb back her hair. Her hands and knees were still somewhat shaky from the lack of food, and once she got dizzy again and had to sit down. Finally, however, she managed to pull on her jacket and deposit Will in the pocket.

Getting downstairs, she discovered, was even harder. Once again she had to sit down to recruit her strength and overcome dizziness. However, she could hear Miss Wingate's voice below and the sound of the door opening and closing. She held tightly to the banister as she continued down.

To her disappointment, the entrance hall was empty when she arrived at the foot of the stairs. When the footman opened the door for her and she stepped outside, she could see a carriage rolling down the driveway. Fortunately, though, the bedraggled group from the orchard rounded the corner of the house and walked toward her.

"Jennifer!" exclaimed Alexandra in alarm. "What are you doing out of bed?"

"Uncle!" Jennifer called, sitting down abruptly on the front step. "I need to tell you something!"

Browning hurried over to her and bent down to listen to what she was saying. His eyes lighted up, and he called to the groom who had just brought round the carriage to bring his curricle to the front immediately.

"What is happening?" demanded Michael. "Jenny, what did you tell Uncle?"

As their uncle was explaining what Jennifer had overheard, Ned and Clarissa and Rupert arrived in the pony cart and the groom raced around the corner in the curricle.

"Can we go, too?" demanded Ned, holding the ribbons of the pony cart.

"Most certainly you may. Isobel, you get in the pony cart, too," he commanded his niece. Handing Alexandra into the curricle, he gave her Jennifer to hold on her lap, and Michael jumped onto the groom's perch. "Follow me!" he commanded Ned, and the pair trotted swiftly down the drive, Toby doing his best to keep pace with the elegant gray pair pulling the curricle.

Alistair Trumbull was still watching sadly from the window. "It's all been too much for the poor fellow," he told his wife. "The robbery, the breaking off of the engagement." He shook his head and poured himself a brandy as consolation.

CHAPTER 23

Miss Wingate's carriage—or rather Browning's carriage, in which Miss Wingate and her mother were riding—slowed as it approached the tollgate. Suddenly, however, it lurched to an abrupt halt. Sylvester, displeased by life in general as well as by the tumbling of his cage onto the floor, yowled noisily.

"Good afternoon, ladies. I hear that you have a cat accompanying you on your journey."

Mrs. Wingate paled and clutched her handkerchief to her mouth as a gentleman in a bright blue riding coat opened the door next to her. A black silk mask covered his face.

"Who are you?" she asked, her voice quavering. "What do you want with us?"

"Never fear, my lady," he responded comfortingly. "We will slow you for only a minute or two."

Outside, the driver was facing a man with a pistol, as was the footman.

"This is outrageous!" said Miss Wingate. "This is a public road!"

The man in the blue coat nodded. "It is indeed, ma'am," he responded genially, "and I am a member of the public."

He was just reaching into the carriage, leaning over Sylvester's cage, when the cat struck at his arm. His hand was gloved, but his movement had exposed a slender strip of skin between sleeve and glove, and the cat's aim was impeccable. He cursed and jerked back his hand while Mrs. Wingate smiled grimly. Sylvester, after all, had his points.

Before he could try again, a shot rang out and he stepped back from the carriage to assess the situation. A curricle was rapidly approaching, and his two henchmen were pulling back from the carriage.

The tollgate keeper, who had been cowering inside his small cottage, was emboldened by the sound of reinforcements and emerged with a pistol. At that, the two henchmen faded from the scene entirely.

When Browning arrived, he handed the ribbons to Michael and leaped down, hurrying over to the carriage.

"Are you quite all right?" he asked Pamela and her mother.

"No thanks to you!" snapped Pamela. "Drive on!" she cried to the coachman, who looked down at his master questioningly.

"You may leave in just a moment," said Browning, smiling at them as he picked up Sylvester's travel basket, the one in which he had arrived at Greengage. As Jennifer's words had led him to suspect, the basket was extremely heavy.

He pulled it out, closed the door, and waved to the coachman to drive on. Outraged once more, Pamela put her head out the window.

"That belongs to Vincent!" she cried. "I shall tell him that you took it!"

Browning waved to her. "By all means, do so!" he called. "And give your cousin my regards."

The man in the blue coat looked at the basket and shook his head. "It is a pity that I was no faster," he observed. "Would you mind raising the lid, sir, so that I may see just what I am missing?"

Browning raised it and the other man whistled in admiration.

"This was not a fortunate day for me."

"Jack?" Michael had hopped down from the curricle and come close to the pair. "Is that you?"

"Indeed it is, dear boy," was the reply. "And I am pleased to see you again—although I wish it were under happier circumstances."

"Why, you're the highwayman—Gentleman Jack," said Alexandra in wonder as she too approached.

Again he bowed. "And I am pleased to see you in such health, Miss Lytton. I would like to thank you for caring for my protégé after—after his unfortunate accident on the road."

"You mean after you abandoned him on the highway," said Alexandra dryly.

"Just so—but then I knew that I was leaving him in the hands of a good Samaritan," he said blithely.

"I might just as easily have turned him in to the magistrate," she pointed out.

"But you didn't," he replied, "and I knew that you wouldn't."

"And so this was your highwayman?" inquired Browning, looking at his nephew, and Michael nodded.

A brief conversation with Gentleman Jack revealed his brief association with Vincent Wingate. He had met that gentleman after holding him up one evening. When he discovered that Wingate had nothing worth stealing, their conversation had turned to those who did.

"He knew that his cousin had just become engaged to you and that you had a goodly house in the neighborhood. I thought perhaps I should rob it straightaway, but he advised me to wait until the grand party when the house would be filled with guests—and with jewels."

Jack smiled at them, quite as though he was explaining an everyday occurrence—which, of course, it was for him. He had removed his mask, which he said had grown too warm, and seated himself on a stone beside the road.

"I have been keeping my eye upon the manor house—and upon all of you. Though I must say that I was astonished that it happened to be *your* house," he said, smiling at Michael.

"But that didn't stop you from robbing us," observed Browning dryly.

"Naturally not," agreed the highwayman with dignity. "This was a matter of business."

The pony cart had rolled up by then, and Browning, denying Ned and Rupert the pleasure of a closer acquaintance with an actual highwayman, escorted them all home, carrying the basket of jewels and leaving Gentleman Jack in the charge of the tollgate keeper to await orders from the local magistrate.

"Now, Miss Lytton," said Browning later that same day after he had summoned her to the library. "We need to have a talk that I have been longing for."

"Indeed?" she asked coolly, although her heart was beating unusually fast. "I should imagine that everything is quite settled. The children are to stay with you at Greengage, you are to engage a governess and a tutor. I should be happy to make recommendations for you before I leave."

"Would you indeed?" he asked, his winged brows rising as he moved closer to her. "Just what recommendations would you make?"

"Well, I know of several people who would make very satisfactory instructors for the children," she told him, backing away as he moved closer.

"I cannot think that they would meet my special requirements," he observed, moving still closer as she backed away more rapidly.

It was, she thought, very difficult to maintain an appropriate degree of dignity as one backed up rapidly. Indeed, she discovered suddenly that her heel was striking an immovable object. She could move no farther back.

She decided that staring at his chin rather than looking him in the eye was advisable. "And just what special requirements are you speaking of, Mr. Browning?" she inquired in her best governess voice.

He put his hand beneath her chin and lifted it so that she was looking into dark, smiling eyes. "I am amazed that you must ask, Miss Lytton. We require a special blend of the Amazon—and the hedgehog."

In spite of her intention to maintain a certain dignity in this interview with her employer, she felt laughter bubbling up. It was cut off suddenly, however, as Mr. Browning drew closer still.

The library door had been just slightly ajar and Michael had been watching the scene carefully. When he saw his uncle take Miss Lytton firmly in his arms, he closed the door, turned to his brother and sisters, and grinned.

"I believe that we have an aunt!" he informed them, grinning.

The two in the library looked at each other when a sudden gleeful shouting rose in the entrance hall, punctuated by brief, sharp terrier barks.

"I believe that is an announcement of your acceptance into the family, my dear," he murmured, drawing her close once more.

In the entrance hall the children were holding an impromptu ball, with even Ned entering into the dance. Butterworth watched them indulgently, and smiled when the dormouse skittered across the floor in pursuit of a hazelnut that had slipped from Ned's pocket. In the kitchen, Mrs. Melling was happily removing a plum cake from the oven, certain that she would soon be receiving a visit from the children—led by Ned and Rupert.

It was a very pleasant thing, she informed Betty, to be cooking for a family once more. When the greengages were ripe this year, she would put up extra jam for the winter. She smiled as she worked. It had been a very long time since Greengage Manor had been a home.

EPILOGUE

Richard Browning lay stretched on the grass, a stack of greengage plums in a basket next to him.

"Come now, Uncle! You can't just lie there all day and wait for the plums to drop down to you! You have to pick them!"

Michael was sitting on a limb of a nearby tree, looking down at him.

"Nonsense!" replied Browning. "I shall wait for them to come to me. I see absolutely no point in putting myself out as you are. You shall be exhausted before you ever enter Sandhurst."

Michael had finally decided that he would like to attend a military academy and take a commission in the cavalry afterward, so soon he would be leaving them.

He tossed a plum in Michael's direction. "I shall expect you to teach Ned and Alex how to fence, you know. We will expect you home with regularity."

Michael grinned. "And I will be here. But I don't think that you truly want Ned to learn how to use a sword properly. Just think what you will be unleashing on the world."

"Your point is well taken," replied Browning. Ned, who had outgrown the pony cart and graduated to riding a hunter and driving a curricle, was a force to be reckoned with—as was Rupert, who still attended him everywhere.

Isobel had had her first Season and declined several proposals, deciding that she would wait until she was absolutely certain of her heart, and Clarissa was attending a nearby academy for young ladies, studying Latin and Greek and Italian and French.

He looked up as Alexandra walked toward him down the green alley between the greengage trees, with Alex tumbling along behind her in leading strings. On the blanket close by him stretched Jennifer, who had not yet chosen to leave Greengage for school. Next to her stretched Rupert, sleeping, and on his back stretched Will, lazy in the afternoon sun.

As Alexandra approached, Browning rose and took her in his arms, handing the leading strings to Jennifer.

"I cannot resist, my dear. Shall we dance?"

Closing their eyes, they waltzed once more beneath the greengage trees as their children watched, smiling.

ABOUT THE AUTHOR

Mona Gedney lives with her family in Indiana and is the author of thirteen Zebra Regency romances. She is working on her next, ON THE TWELFTH DAY OF CHRISTMAS, to be published in October 2004. Mona loves to hear from readers and you may write to her c/o Zebra Books. Please include a self-addressed stamped envelope if you wish a response.

BOOK YOUR PLACE ON OUR WEBSITE AND MAKE THE READING CONNECTION!

We've created a customized website just for our very special readers, where you can get the inside scoop on everything that's going on with Zebra, Pinnacle and Kensington books.

When you come online, you'll have the exciting opportunity to:

- View covers of upcoming books

- Read sample chapters

- Learn about our future publishing schedule (listed by publication month *and author*)

- Find out when your favorite authors will be visiting a city near you

- Search for and order backlist books from our online catalog

- Check out author bios and background information

- Send e-mail to your favorite authors

- Meet the Kensington staff online

- Join us in weekly chats with authors, readers and other guests

- Get writing guidelines

- AND MUCH MORE!

Visit our website at
http://www.kensingtonbooks.com